NEED

_____

OLIVIA T. TURNER

www.OliviaTTurner.com

Edited by Karen Collins Editing
Cover Design by Olivia T. Turner

COME AND JOIN MY PRIVATE FACEBOOK GROUP!

Become an OTT Lover!

www.facebook.com/groups/OTTLovers

BECOME OBSESSED WITH OTT

Sign up to my mailing list for all the latest OTT news and get a free book that you can't find anywhere else!

OBSESSED
By Olivia T. Turner
A Mailing List Exclusive!

When I look out my office window and see her in the next building, I know I have to have her.

I buy the whole damn company she works for just to be near her.

She's going to be in my office working under me.

Under, over, sideways—we're going to be working together in *every* position.

This young innocent girl is going to find out that I work my employees *hard*.

And that her new rich CEO is already beyond *obsessed* with her.

This dominant and powerful CEO will have you begging for over-time! Is it just me or is there nothing better than a hot muscular alpha in a suit and tie!

All my books are SAFE with zero cheating and a guaranteed sweet HEA. Enjoy!

Go to www.OliviaTTurner.com to get your free ebook of Obsessed

This one is dedicated to my bridesmaid and longtime friend Megan. Deny it all you want dirty girl, I saw you at my wedding sneaking into the coat check with my cousin.
This one is for you…

CHAPTER ONE

Violet

"IS THAT HOW YOU'RE WEARING YOUR HAIR?" BECKY ASKS ME when all of the other bridesmaids are distracted with the champagne.

She's got that sour look on her face. The one that makes her look like a ferret.

"I thought you said you were going to try and look *decent* for my wedding. Are you *trying* to ruin all of the wedding photos?"

She's shaking her head as she looks down at me.

This is going to be my new stepmother.

In a few hours.

This monster is going to be in my family.

I still can't believe it. I'll never understand what my father was thinking when he asked her to marry him.

She's a horrible person and this wedding is bringing out the worst in her.

If there was a UFC for the world's worst bridezillas, Becky would be reigning champion.

Tears start to prickle my eyes as she steps back and looks me up and down with a disapproving look on her stern face.

"And you promised you were going to lose some weight. What happened with that? Did you go to McDonald's instead of the gym?"

I feel my cheeks getting hot as I look down at my purple bridesmaid dress. Maybe I'm a little thick, but I'm not horrible looking enough to ruin a wedding.

The worst part is that I *did* try to lose weight because I knew she would resent me if I wasn't as stick thin as her other bridesmaids. And for another reason... Ashton is going to be at the wedding.

"You begged us to pay for a gym membership and you don't even use it," she says, shaking her head in disgust. "When I move in with you and Thomas, there's going to be a lot of changes, Violet. *A lot* of changes."

"I didn't beg you," I whisper under my breath.

Her cruel eyes snap back up to mine. "What?"

I didn't. I didn't even ask. I came home from school one day and there was a gym membership on my desk. It was in my name and there was a note beside it that said:

I'd rather you walk down the aisle rather than waddle down it.
You have 12 months paid.
Do everyone a favor and use it.
- Becky

I showed it to my father, but he just shrugged and said that she wants the wedding to be perfect, that she's trying her best to make that happen and that he'll talk to her.

A whole lot of good it did. Becky is great at turning on the sweetness and charms when my father is around, but as soon as he leaves the room, she's all scowls and rolling eyes.

She absolutely loathes me and wants me out of the house. She'll be moving in next week as my father's wife. I just turned eighteen and I can tell that my days in that house are numbered. She's going to do everything she can to get me out of there.

"What did you say?" she repeats. She's staring at me with a challenging look, begging me to say something to set her off.

I just grin at her. "Nothing. *Mom.*"

Her nostrils flare and her eyes harden as I walk past her. She hates it when I call her that. In her eyes, she's still a hot twenty-one-year-old, and I guess everyone else is too afraid to tell her that those days ended about twenty years ago.

The wedding coordinator rushes in, looking stressed out as usual. We're all getting ready in the suite of the hotel while the guests arrive at the reception area down below.

"We're at T-minus ten minutes," the wedding coordinator says as she frantically looks over her clipboard. The poor girl is sweating.

If Becky is meaner to one person in this world, it's probably her. The wedding coordinator is terrified of making even the slightest mistake and incurring Becky's wrath.

"Have some champagne!" Sheila, the redheaded bridesmaid says as she skips over with a few glasses in her hand. Her cheeks are flushed and she's smiling as she hands me one. I think she's already had too many.

"What kind is that?" Becky asks as she looks over at the bottle. "Moet and Chandon? Ugh. I only drink Crystal."

"More for me," Sheila says as she raises her eyebrows at me.

"No," Becky snaps. "You've already had enough. I'm

going for traditional and classy, not plastered and trashy. Put the glass down."

Sheila stuffs one into my hand and then puts the others on the dresser. Her group of friends were the mean girls in high school and big surprise, Becky was the queen bee. They're in their early forties and they still do whatever she says.

I go to take a sip and Becky rips the glass out of my hand. "Aren't you underage? I'm sure with that extra weight you can handle the alcohol, but just in case, I don't want you tripping while you're walking down the aisle. Violet is the most *clumsiest* person I've ever met. I bet she takes after her mother, because her father is anything but clumsy. He is a rockstar in the bedroom."

My stomach churns as all of the other girls cheer.

"Five minutes," the wedding coordinator says, looking increasingly agitated.

I walk over to her and pretend to look at the itinerary. "Is the best man here yet?" I whisper to her. "He was coming in from London."

"Mr. Ashton?" she says with her eyes lighting up. I should have known that she would have noticed him. He's got the type of dark eyes that demand your attention. "Yes, he's here."

My heart starts to pound a little faster. He's here. Ashton Sparks is here.

Becky can tear me down all she wants, but she can't ruin this.

I've been waiting to see him for four years. Four *long* years.

The last time I saw him was at my mother's funeral. I was fourteen and already in love. I've been in love with him for my entire life.

He picked me up at the cemetery and held me close to his chest as everyone cried. I can still remember the soothing sound of his heart beating, the sweet smell of the rose on his jacket, the feeling like everything was going to be okay while I was in his arms even though my whole world was crashing down around me.

And then he moved.

I was heartbroken. Devastated.

He left to London for work and I never saw him again.

My friends cycled through crushes on a weekly basis. Boys in the class, movie stars, musicians, the occasional teacher, the lifeguard at the pool. Not me. I've only had eyes for one man and he was across the Atlantic ocean from me.

My father met Ashton in college and they've been best friends ever since. I don't know how many times I've looked at the pictures from their college days that my father had tucked away in the basement. They're all curled up at the edges and worn out, but it's not from time, it's from a teenage Violet rubbing her fingertips over his arms and kissing his face while wishing it was the real thing.

My father visited him from time to time in London, and I always begged him to take me but he never did.

"It's going to be boring," he would say.

Like spending time with Ashton could ever be boring.

I was a little girl the last time he saw me, but I'm eighteen now. Most people would say that he's way too old for me, but I don't agree. I've always belonged to him, even if he's never known it.

I'm wondering where he is now. What he's doing. What he looks like in his suit. If he's still as sexy as I remember...

"Get your head out of the clouds, Violet," Becky says as she walks past me. She bumps her elbow into my breast as she passes. "And try not to ruin this for me."

She hates me because my dad loves me. I guess she feels threatened by my existence and she's doing what bitches do when they feel threatened: they get their claws out.

I just stare forward with a nervous excitement radiating through my body as the wedding coordinator lines us up.

She brings us downstairs and we see the groomsmen waiting in the hall. They're all there except for my father and Ashton. I have to walk down the aisle to them.

I know that I'll be fantasizing that I'm the bride and I'm walking down the aisle to him. It will be bittersweet once I get to the top and have to face that he's here for my father and not for me.

I take a deep breath as my cousin Doug takes a hold of my arm. "Looking good, cuz."

"You too. I didn't think you'd ever take that Metallic t-shirt off."

"I'm wearing it under my shirt," he says with a grin.

"*Shhhh*," Becky hisses from the back of the line.

"What's with Bridezilla?" Doug whispers.

I try to stifle my laugh, but it doesn't work. "Bridezilla got her head chopped off by a much more heinous monster: Beckyzilla."

We both laugh as the wedding coordinator opens the doors. The music starts and she waves me and Doug forward into the packed reception hall.

I take a deep breath and start walking.

CHAPTER TWO

Ashton

"Look at the turnout," I say as I look around at the packed reception hall. "They must be all on your new bride's side. I know an asshole like you couldn't draw a crowd like this."

My best friend Thomas laughs. "You came all the way from London to be by my side."

"Yeah, but I'm an asshole too. Us assholes have to stick together."

He laughs as he slaps his hand on my back.

"Thanks for coming, buddy."

"I wouldn't miss it for the world." I've been living in London for the past four years, but my best friend is still and will always be Thomas. I'm thrilled to be standing next to him today as his best man.

"But seriously," I say as more people come in. "Who are all of these people? Does Becky have a huge family?"

He shakes his head as he waves at someone in the third row. "Not even. Hardly anyone from her family even came."

That's odd. I haven't met her yet and I trust Thomas' judgment, but there's something kind of off when a bride's family doesn't even come to her wedding.

Thomas is a rich man and I don't want him to be taken advantage of. He's always had a blindspot with women. I can still remember his slutty second girlfriend who offered me a blowjob at his house while he was making her a sandwich in the kitchen. He thought he was going to marry that one.

Luckily, he found his true love, Pam. My chest tightens when I remember her funeral and how his adorable little girl was clinging onto me like she never wanted to let me go.

I push away the sad thoughts and put a smile on my face. This is a happy day. My best friend is in love again and hopefully, it's to another great woman.

"This is all my company," he whispers to me as he winks at someone in the crowd. "I had to invite all three hundred and sixteen of them *and* their spouses."

"Wow," I say as I look around. I have over four hundred employees in my company and I've never even had lunch with one of them.

"I keep telling them we're a family," he whispers. "It's kind of hard to keep saying that after I didn't invite them to my wedding."

I laugh as I slap his back. Thomas always was a big softie.

"How's Violet?" I ask, thinking back to the way she smelled when I held her in my arms. She was so cute and innocent. I always loved that girl. "Does she get along with Becky?"

"Oh yeah," he says with a nod. "They're like best friends."

I tilt my head as I look at him with a raised eyebrow. "Really?"

He sighs. "It could be better." He looks at his watch and straightens up. "It's going to start any second now."

The piano starts playing and everyone goes quiet. "Good luck," I whisper.

Suddenly, the double doors fly open and everyone turns around with a gasp.

The smile slowly fades from my face when Violet appears.

This is not the young goofy girl I remember. She's all grown up and the beautiful sight of her in that purple dress is preventing me from breathing.

My whole body is tight and my heart is beating a mile a minute as I watch her. She looks right at me and the sight of her gorgeous blue eyes locked onto mine make my legs buckle.

I hold onto Thomas for support as she turns away with her cheeks blushing. She looks at the crowd on the left and then on the right, smiling shyly the entire time.

I can't believe it. I'm stunned.

This is Thomas' daughter? This is the girl who used to ride her pink bike up and down his driveway whenever I came over? The girl who asked me to marry her when she was only nine-years-old?

If I knew she would have turned out like this, I would have said yes immediately.

Her eyes make their way back to mine and her cheeks redden even more when we make eye contact. It feels like she's reaching in through my chest and clenching my soul.

My hands are squeezed into fists by my side. Every cell in my body is screaming at me to rush down the aisle and take her. To throw her over my shoulder and bring her back to London.

It takes every last ounce of restraint I have to keep my feet planted on the floor.

Her beautiful brown hair is styled up with baby's breath flowers pinned all around, making her look like she just dropped out of heaven. My eyes drink up every inch of her young supple body from her bare neck and shoulders down to her curvy hips. She has big tits and more curves than the skinny bridesmaids behind her. She's so fucking perfect. I can't even handle it.

I'm finally able to rip my eyes away from her to glare at the guy on her arm. An edgy, twitchy feeling starts to take over my body when I see her hand gripping his bicep. I don't want her touching anyone but me. It's making my pulse race. It's causing a pounding in my ears.

Thomas leans over and whispers to me while I'm picturing taking this guy's head and snapping his neck in front of everyone to see. Then they'd all know that this girl is mine and not to be touched.

"That's my beautiful girl," Thomas whispers. "Isn't she— Holy shit, Ashton! Are you okay?"

I'm so fucking far from okay.

I feel like I just shattered and only she can pick up the pieces.

My body is trembling and my face is probably as red as the rose on my lapel.

Then I recognize the kid. *Thank god.*

My breath comes back. My chest loosens a bit.

I still don't like him touching her, but it's better knowing that he's her cousin. It's Derek or Donny or Doug or something like that.

"Ashton," Thomas whispers as she approaches. She's so close. I inhale deep, trying to smell her, but I can't. She's too far away. "Do you need to sit down?"

I don't answer. I *can't* answer. I can't talk. I can't do anything but stare.

They walk up the steps and Thomas takes his attention off me to step forward and kiss her cheek.

I don't stop staring at her even as her cousin steps beside

me and playfully hits my arm. He says something that I don't hear over the pounding in my ears.

One couple after another come up, but my eyes are locked on the young teenage beauty across the alter from me.

Violet is smiling as she watches the bridesmaids join her, but it's a tight smile. The adorable little lines around her eyes aren't there and I can't see her white teeth. Every few seconds her eyes flitter on me, but as soon as she sees me staring, they dart away.

She's pretending like she doesn't notice, but her cheeks are blushing. She knows I'm looking. Wanting her. *Needing* her.

The music changes and everyone stands up. There's a change of energy in the air as the bride enters the room.

I don't even look. I don't think I'm physically capable of peeling my eyes off of this stunning girl.

Everyone is facing the entrance of the room, but me. I'm turned and staring at the only person that matters. The woman that will be *my* future bride one day.

The bride arrives and Thomas takes her hand.

I let out a low huff of frustration as they block my view. I quickly step to the side and breathe a little easier when I have Violet back in my sights.

A small part of me wonders if I'm being too obvious. If the over five hundred guests can see me staring, salivating, lusting over this girl, but the bigger part of me doesn't care. The uncivilized part of me is in control now. She's sparked something primal within me. My barbarian genes have come alive.

The minister starts droning on, but I don't hear one word. I'm too busy thinking of how I can steal this girl and bring her back to London with me. Would they let me get on the plane with a screaming and kicking girl over my shoulder?

The need to claim her is growing like a monster within me. I want to rip off that purple dress and sink my raw cock into her young juicy cunt. There's no way I'm taking this girl with a condom. It's going to be all natural and unprotected. The skin of my cock will be sliding against her soft pussy walls without anything preventing me from breeding her young womb.

Once I impregnate her, she'll be in my life for good. In London, over here—it doesn't matter. As long as her pussy curves to my dick and her stomach is round with my child, we'll be fine.

Just thinking about sliding into that ripe cunt gets me rock hard. *Shit.* There are more than five hundred people looking up here and I have a raging hard-on.

I shift and try to turn away to hide it, but it's like trying to hide a two-by-four. It's sticking straight up and demanding attention. It knows what it wants and it's not ashamed to announce it to everyone.

Time seems to warp all around me. I'm no longer in the same reality as everyone else. My reality revolves around Violet. She's all that matters in my world.

Some minutes drag by incredibly slow and some flick by in the beat of a thumping heart, but for every single moment, I'm staring at my girl.

I don't hear a word from the minister, just a deep rumbling in my pounding ears, so I don't notice when he starts talking to me.

Thomas turns and slaps my shoulder and I finally snap out of it. I look at him in shock and everyone starts laughing.

He has his hand outstretched.

I'm so confused. I can't think straight. It's like this girl has rewired my brain. She's taken everything out and replaced it with obsession and need.

"The ring?" Thomas says with a chuckle.

Oh, right.

I quickly pat my pockets as everyone laughs again. I find it inside my jacket pocket and pull it out with trembling hands. My palms are so sweaty and they leave streaks on the felt bag.

My best friend looks at me funny as he takes the ring from my hand and turns back around.

He's putting the ring on his bride's finger, but my eyes are already back on his daughter.

Violet is looking at me, but her eyes dart away the second I turn back to her. She smiles as she watches the exchanging of the rings with blushing cheeks.

The minister tells them to kiss and finally, this fucking thing is over.

Everyone cheers as they walk down the steps with their hands in the air.

Before they even make it down to the aisle I go to her.

CHAPTER THREE

Ashton

MY HEART IS POUNDING AS I RACE UP TO HER.

I don't know what to say. All I know is that I want her to be mine. That I need to be as close to her blushing cheeks and soft pink lips as possible.

She swallows hard and looks up at me with her gorgeous blue eyes.

"Hi, Ashton," she says shyly.

There's a lump in my throat. My whole body is stirring and craving a touch.

She's even more perfect up close. Her blue eyes are as bright as an iceberg under the Arctic waters and as warm as the sun in the desert. Her long eyelashes flutter up and down as she looks up at me with a hint of nerves racing through her young body.

I'm going to die if I don't have her soon. My pounding heart is going to give out. It can't keep up this pace for long.

"You look…"

What can I say? There are no words to describe how beautiful she is. Shakespeare himself would have given up the pen if he ever had to describe her beauty. How can you describe perfection? You can't. You just stare at it in awe and that's exactly what I'm doing

"Watch out," Doug says as he pushes past me. "She's mine, dude."

I watch in horror as he wraps his arm around hers. This is it. It's over. Five hundred people are going to watch me take this fucker's neck and turn it in the wrong direction.

Just as I'm stepping forward with an uncontrollable rage creeping into my body, an arm grabs mine. I whip my head around and see the maid of honor smiling at me.

"You're with me," she says with a lick of her lips. She's giving me some serious fuck me eyes, but right now being with anyone but Violet is the last thing on my mind. I don't think I'll ever be interested in another girl again.

Doug and Violet head down the steps, leaving me in shock.

"I'm Nikki," the girl on my arm says as she leans into me. Her hard breasts press up against my bicep and I immediately move away from her. "I heard all about you. Did you hear about me?"

"No."

We start walking down the steps and my eyes are locked on Violet's bare back. I don't like that she has her arm wrapped around that guy's arm, but the only thing keeping me in check is knowing that it's her cousin.

"I'm surprised that my reputation didn't get around," she whispers playfully. Her perfume smells like vanilla and cotton candy. It's making me nauseous. Everything about this girl is making me nauseous. "I think I'm staying in the room across from yours. Room 508."

She's laying it on pretty thick, but I just turn away.

I just want Violet. I want her so bad.

My eyes roam down her back to her curvy ass that looks so fucking good in that purple dress. I start imagining hiking it up and discovering that she's not wearing any panties over that sweet young pussy underneath, and my cock hardens to the point of pain.

Everyone is looking at us and smiling as we walk down the aisle. I can't smile back. I can't even fake it. Not with all of these eyes on her.

They're looking at what's mine and I don't like it. I want to blind each and everyone one of them for daring to drag their eyes over her curves.

"Fuck," I mutter under my breath.

This is just the beginning. She's a bridesmaid and part of the show.

Everyone will be looking at her all night. Touching her. Kissing her.

It feels like a weight drops onto my heavy shoulders.

This is going to be the longest fucking night of my life.

CHAPTER FOUR

Violet

A BEAUTIFUL WEIGHTLESS FEELING IS FLOWING THROUGH MY tingling body as the photographer snaps photos of us.

"Can I have everyone looking over *here?*" he snaps with a huff of annoyance in his breath.

He's trying to take pictures of the bridal party, but Ashton is ruining his plans. Every single wedding photo that my dad and Becky will have will be with Ashton staring right at me.

My lips curl up into a grin as I feel his heated eyes on me. I love it.

He was staring at me the entire ceremony like he was going to rush over and start ripping off my clothes at any moment. A part of me wanted him to.

I love having his eyes on me. I want all of his attention.

"Over here," the photographer says as he snaps his fingers in frustration. He's getting increasingly annoyed with Ashton and I grin happily, knowing that I'm the cause of it.

"Who's not looking at the goddamn camera?!?" Becky snaps.

It almost makes me forget that my father just married a cunt like Becky.

Ashton turns to the photographer and I feel a sense of loss radiating through me now that his eyes aren't on me anymore.

I sneak a quick peek at him between photos and see everyone smiling but him. His jaw is clenched and his hands are squeezed into fists at his sides.

"All right, thank you," the photographer says as he hooks the camera strap around his shoulder and lets it fall by his side. "Just the bride and groom now. Maybe by the water."

We're outside of the beautiful hotel's reception hall on the grass by the water. Boats are drifting down the river and waving at the bride and groom as they approach. My dad waves back. Becky doesn't. She's too busy complaining about them ruining her shot. As if she owns the entire river…

It's a beautiful sunny summer afternoon with a nice breeze that keeps it from getting too hot, which is good because my afternoon is about to get a lot hotter.

Ashton comes up to me once again. He towers over me with his big powerful body.

"Violet."

The way he says my name in that deep growly voice sends warm shivers racing through my body.

"You're all grown up."

He looks me up and down and the warm shivers turn into a swirling heat that settles between my legs.

"I just turned eighteen-years-old."

I want him to know that I'm legal. Barely legal, but legal enough for whatever those dark lust-filled eyes have planned. I hold his heated gaze and the thick air between us gets charged with a raw and primal need. My heart is pounding when I finally turn away.

"Are you enjoying London?"

He nods. "Yes, but something tells me it's going to feel very empty when I return."

I lick my lips as I quickly look him over. He looks so gorgeous in his tuxedo. The navy blue sleeves hug his big strong arms and broad shoulders. I just want to climb up him like a tree and slide down on that hard cock that's sticking up against the inside of his pants.

"That's too bad," I say with a tilt of my head. "Is there something you can take back with you to fill up the empty void?"

He's staring down at me with his sexy hazel eyes. His salt and pepper hair is combed to the side and I can't help but think that he would make an excellent James Bond.

"There's something," he answers in a low voice. "But I might have to drag her back with me."

"You might be surprised. I think anyone would love to go to London with you."

We stare at each other for a long moment. I hope he knows what I meant, but from the way he's fixated on me, I think that he does.

I've been in love with this man for as long as I can remember, but I've never been able to do a damn thing about it.

He's always looked at me like the child I was, but things are different now. Finally, they're different.

I'm a woman now and he's finally looking at me like someone to desire. Someone that he can have.

I just don't want to share him. I want to be his one and only.

My stomach flutters with nerves, but I have to ask him. I don't know if I want to hear the answer, but I have to ask the question.

"Are you married, or a… girlfriend?" A lump gets stuck in my throat with that last word.

He shakes his head with a viciousness that tells me he's

not lying. It's like he's disgusted to even think about himself with another woman. I hope it's because he's thinking about me.

"There's no one," he says as he takes a step forward. "Only you."

My lips drop open in shock as he takes my hand in his.

He starts to lean forward and I think that he might kiss me when my aunt grabs my arm and pulls me away.

"Sorry, Ashton," she says with an apologetic smile. "I just want to grab Violet here for a second. Violet, you have to meet my new boyfriend. I've told him all about you."

I turn back and look at Ashton as she drags me across the lawn, babbling the entire way. He's breathing heavily as he stares back at me with shining eyes.

Questions keep racing through my head.

Was he talking about me going back to London with him? Was he going to kiss me?

What's going to happen next?

I'm surrounded by my cousins and they're all laughing and joking around as they drink their cocktails. I'm holding the cold glass in my aching fingers, but I'm not laughing. I keep glancing over my shoulder at Ashton to see if he's still looking at me.

He is. He always is.

He's leaning on the bar looking gorgeous in his tux as he sips on a beer. He doesn't even take his eyes off me as he raises the pint glass to his lips and takes a sip.

I turn back to my cousins, feeling all lightheaded and tingling.

All of their attention is on me. "What?"

They all laugh.

"What's with you, V?" Gemma asks. "You're a total space cadet today."

"Sorry," I say feeling embarrassed. "I don't know what's come over me."

My pussy aches as I glance back at Ashton. One of my uncles is talking to him, but he doesn't seem to be paying Uncle Michael any mind. All of his attention is on me. Right where I like it.

Ashton has been best friends with my father forever so he knows my family well. I've noticed that people keep coming up to him with smiles, but after a few quick harsh words from him, they scurry away with their tails between their legs.

It's like he can't take his focus off of me for even a second.

I'm too shy to go over, so I walk around the room, saying hi to the guests. I'm intensely aware of his eyes on me the entire time.

And I love it.

Wait until he finds out that I've saved myself for him.

Not only am I a virgin, but I've never even kissed another boy before. I've had the opportunity but it always felt too wrong. It felt like I was cheating. Like I was betraying the man in my life who I knew would one day be mine.

So I kept my legs closed and my lips sealed. For him.

The wait was agonizingly long and painful, but hopefully, it will be over tonight.

CHAPTER FIVE

Violet

"THANK YOU," I SAY TO THE WAITER AS HE POURS MY WINE. I'M sitting at the long head table next to my cousin Doug, who is somewhere at the bar.

We're on a little platform overlooking all of the guests in the reception hall. It's a beautiful set up with huge center-pieces of white flowers and candles. There's nice music playing and soft lighting as everyone gets settled for dinner.

My new stepmother might be a total cunt, but at least she has nice taste when it comes to decorating. It certainly cost my father enough money. He only wanted a small thing with close family, but she insisted that her wedding be a lavish affair with everyone they knew invited to see how amazing she was.

It's like she can hear my thoughts because she gets up from her chair and walks over. She's got an icy smile on her face that gives me cold shivers.

"The daughter I never wanted," she says, smiling as she

puts her hand on the back of my chair. To anyone in the crowd, she looks so sweet and nice with her fake smile and tilted head. If only they knew how vile she really was. "Is it too late to put you up for adoption?"

I smile back at her. "Is it too late to tell my dad that you're a money-grubbing whore?"

Her fake smile withers into a scowl and she leaves.

I glance over at Ashton's chair. It's still empty. I haven't seen him in a while and it's making me think that maybe he isn't as interested in me as I thought he was.

I haven't even talked to him since my aunt pulled me away.

All of the emotions start building up inside me and I need a breather. I get up from the table and sneak out the side door. The terrace and grassy area are empty except for an old dude from my dad's company who's smoking a cigarette. I smile at him and walk around the building, holding my arms. The sun is just starting to set and it's the perfect summer evening. Perfect weather-wise. In every other area, it's falling apart.

I should be upset because my father married that woman, but I'm actually upset because I seem to have lost Ashton's attention.

Boy, was I wrong.

Ashton comes rushing around the building and he grabs my arm. I gasp as he pushes me up against the wall and holds me there with his big strong hands.

I can feel my heartbeat thundering through me as he towers over me. There's no one around. There's no one to see. He can do *anything* to me right now.

His eyes are on my parted lips as he gently slides his hand up my jaw.

My heart is pounding furiously in my chest as I feel his warm breath tickling my hot skin. God, my pussy is aching. My body is on fire.

There's so much sexual tension between us, I'm surprised the air isn't rippling with electricity.

"I've been wanting to do this all fucking day. You're torturing me with this purple dress."

My head is back, chin in the air, lips parted. I want him to *take* it.

"This little mouth…" He runs his thumb over my lips and I gasp. "The things I have planned for it."

He marvels and stares at my mouth like it's the most amazing thing in the world. Like he's looking at a precious diamond for the first time or admiring rare rubies.

I'm already breathing hard. The strong hand on my waist that's pinning me to the brick wall is really getting me going. My nipples are firm and aching under my dress. I arch my back and press my breasts up to him, teasing him as I breathe heavily. I want this as much as he does.

"Oh, fuck it." His lips come down on mine and we make out hard. All of the want and need of the past eighteen years of my life come boiling to the surface in this kiss. My hands are wrapped around his head, pulling his mouth to mine. His hands are everywhere. Grabbing at my breasts, my ass, pulling me closer. They're on my cheeks, in my hair, on my back. My pussy is burning. I'm so fucking wet.

All I've ever wanted was for this to happen. And now it's happening and it's better than I imagined.

My hair comes undone, but I don't care. He rips his mouth away from mine and starts kissing my neck. I moan. My back arches. I'm pressing my breasts into his hand and moaning for more. I want to feel him on my skin. I want these strong rough hands scratching against my tingling nipples.

I gasp when I feel how hard he is. His rock hard cock is pressed against my stomach and it makes my pussy burn. I want it inside me. The need is growing. I want to feel it stretching my virgin pussy out.

His lips come crushing back against mine and I moan

when he thrusts his tongue into my mouth. It's so deep. It's so *fucking* good.

A powerful hand grabs the back of my thigh and he lifts my leg up while he pushes his cock against me. I hope he does it right now. I hope he fucks me here.

Someone starts calling his name.

At first we pay it no mind, but the sound becomes clearer.

"Ashton. Ashton? Where is the best man?"

It's the DJ. Shit.

His voice is ringing out through the speakers.

Ashton just curses under his breath, but he keeps kissing me even more frantically. His lips move down to my neck as I grind my hips against his cock.

"Can someone find the best man? It's time for his speech."

I gasp when his mouth drops down to the top of my chest. He's kissing my hot skin, kissing my breasts over my dress, kissing everywhere. He's got a firm grip on my right breast. He pushes it up until my hard nipple pops out and then he takes it into his mouth.

"Fuck," I moan as he swirls his hot tongue around it. *"Holy shit."*

He's not stopping even though the DJ keeps calling him.

"Ashton," I gasp. My hands are in his hair, pulling him closer, fucking his hair all up. "Your speech. You have to go."

"No," he grunts between kisses. His grip on my body tightens and my swollen lips curl up into a smile.

"You have to go. We have all night." My breathless words are telling him to go, but my body is begging him to stay.

"I need more than all night with you. I need you in my life for good. You're my girl now."

"I've always been your girl, Ashton," I say, gasping as his hand slides down my stomach. He cups my burning pussy and I throw my head back and cry out. My whole body is smoldering under his touch.

"Ashton? Where are you, Ashton? Can someone put out an APB on the best man?"

"This fucking guy," he growls. "I'm going to shove that microphone down his throat."

I can't breathe with his hand on me like this. It's over my dress and panties, but still, it's enough to get me digging my nails into his biceps.

"This is my cunt now," he growls into my hair as he pushes me back up against the wall. "You keep it away from all other men."

I nod as his firm hand presses up hard against it. The bottom of his palm is pushing against my throbbing clit and I feel myself starting to come undone.

"I don't want to see you talking to any other men tonight. Got that?"

"Yes!"

Just don't stop. I'll do whatever you want while you're touching me like this.

He starts rocking his palm against me and I cum hard on his hand.

I open my lips to scream but he puts his other hand over my mouth and muffles the sound. I'm digging my nails into his suit jacket and rising up on my toes as the orgasm hits. I'm making strange noises like an animal dying as it tears through me.

He leaves me gasping and clutching onto his thick forearm as my whole world flips on its head. I'm his now. I've always been his, but now I'm *really* his.

This is real.

He gently pushes me back up against the wall and steps back.

Waves of delicious heat are flowing through me. Slamming into my heart. Slamming into my core. I'm tingling all over as he looks me up and down.

"You're so beautiful, Violet."

I smile as I feel my cheeks heat up. He makes me feel so special. So loved.

The warm feeling inside gets a little warmer.

"Ashton? Ashton where are you?"

His hair is a mess. His tie is all crooked and my lipstick is smeared all over his mouth.

He definitely looks like he's been up to no good.

He looks away. "I'll be back."

"Wait." I step up to him and smooth out his sexy salt and pepper hair. I fix his tie and run my hands over his rumpled jacket, feeling his hard muscles underneath.

I rub my thumb over his jaw, taking away most of the lipstick. He looks less guilty now.

The secret is between us.

"Ashhhhtttttooooonnnnnn."

"I'm going to strangle this guy with his microphone wire in front of everyone," he growls.

"It's okay," I say softly as I cup his cheek. "I've waited years for you. I can wait a little bit longer."

He kisses me long and hard and then leaves.

"Fuucccckkkk," I moan as I lean back against the wall. I close my eyes and smile as my warm pussy glows.

"There he is," the DJ says over the speakers and everyone claps. *"We thought you'd never come back to us."*

I smile. That's how I felt too.

I'm so happy I was wrong.

CHAPTER SIX

Ashton

THE SPEECH DOESN'T GO WELL. BIG SURPRISE THERE.

I could barely hold the microphone in my sweaty hands let alone think with the scent of Violet's cunt on my fingers. The sweet ripe scent kept swirling up to my nose and making me crazy.

I forgot all about the speech in my pocket and rambled on about how I was happy that Thomas finally found a woman to grow old with.

At the end, I spat out some words of love, which came out easily. I was just thinking of Violet the entire time.

Everyone clapped when I finished and Thomas gave me a big hug. He's already heavy into the wine and scotch, so I don't think he even noticed that I fucked it up.

Everyone is finishing dinner around me, but I haven't touched my plate. My stomach is all clenched up. I couldn't eat if I tried.

It's making me all scratchy inside that Violet is on the

other side of the table. I lean back in my chair and look at the back of her head to make sure she's still there.

This is quickly getting out of hand. I'm past desire. I'm past captivation. I'm past fixation.

I'm in full-blown obsession territory here and I don't see myself getting out anytime soon.

I *need* this girl.

I need to own her. To consume her fully.

It's all I can fucking think about.

The need to stuff her womb with my seed is making my chest so tight that I can't breathe.

"Why do you keep doing that?"

"Huh?"

Thomas is grinning at me. "Why do you keep leaning back like that? Do you have a bad back?"

"Yeah," I say with a shake of my head. I sit back normally as he starts laughing.

"Probably from when Radford kicked our asses. You remember that?"

I grin as I remember that beat down. We were both on the rugby team in college and pretty much everyone but us sucked.

"Are you kidding?" I answer with a chuckle. "I still have mud in my ears from that game."

"We gave it back to them in folds. Didn't we?"

"I still shiver every time I remember the great Thomas the Tank plowing through their Captain."

We're both laughing and reminiscing about our old days on the rugby team. We were the two bruisers the coach sent in when he wanted us to fuck someone up. Thomas the Tank and Ashton the Anvil.

I'm having a great time with my oldest, closest friend until I realize what I just did with his daughter.

It hits me like a punch in the gut. I just grabbed his

teenage daughter's pussy and made her cum. At the guy's wedding no less. What the fuck kind of friend am I?

My body goes still as I look down at the untouched plate in front of me with guilty eyes.

"Lot's of single women here tonight," he says, hitting my shoulder with his. I'm a big man, but Thomas has always been bigger. He was a monster in his youth, but now he just looks like a big teddy bear with his thick layer of fat from all those Sunday afternoon beers, chips, ice cream, barbecues, and all of the other suburban trappings that get guys like him in middle age.

I've always stayed lean. I hit the gym every morning and crank out a few reps on the punching bag. It's the only thing that keeps my edge from taking over. It's the only thing that keeps me sane.

"What about Nikki?" he whispers as he points to the maid of honor down the table. I take the opportunity to look, but I'm not looking at Nikki. I'm looking at his daughter. "I heard that she can suck an ice cube through a straw."

"No thanks," I say when I sit back in my chair.

"Why? You got a girl waiting for you back in London or something?"

There's no girl back in London. There's never been a girl in London. In the four years I've been there, I've just been throwing myself into my work. I own a sports apparel company and I moved to London to start a European division. I've made millions and I like the job, but that's about it. I haven't met anyone I wanted to date.

Until now.

"So, what is it? Don't tell me you're already impotent. We're not that fucking old."

We both laugh. Everyone who attended his wedding knows that I can still get it as hard as a rock with just one look at his daughter.

"I had my eye on someone else."

Should I tell him how I feel? I look at his big hands and picture them wrapped around my neck. My last sight in this world would be of his thick forearms flexing as he choked the life out of me.

"Who? Sheila? I didn't know you were into redheads."

"It's not Sheila."

I take a long sip of my beer and wonder if it's going to be my last.

"Then who? I'll help you out."

"It's—"

"Time for the father-daughter dance," the DJ spits out into the mic.

Everyone gives out a puppy dog *awwwww* as the spotlights hit Thomas and Violet.

I turn and look at her blushing face. She belongs under spotlights, but I still get the urge to run over to where they're hanging from the ceiling and break them. I don't like everyone's attention on her. I'm a jealous brute and I want her all to myself.

Thomas gets up and takes his daughter's hand. He brings her to the dance floor as some soft music about fathers and daughters starts playing. Cameras are being whipped out everywhere as the guests gather around.

My pulse is racing. A bead of sweat drips down my back.

People are *videotaping* her. A young guy in a gray suit with a scraggly beard catches my eye. I can see what's on the tiny screen. He's filming her a little too close for my liking. When I see him zoom in on Violet's curvy ass, I nearly lose it.

I take the napkin off my lap and squeeze it so hard that my knuckles burn. I can't do anything right now. My girl and my friend are enjoying a special moment and I don't want to ruin it by splattering them with blood. Even if it's what that perverted punk deserves.

The song finishes and everyone claps as Violet stands on

her toes and gives her father a kiss on the cheek. My eyes stay on the guy in the gray suit.

When the song finishes, he leaves to go to the bathroom and I rush down to have a little word with him.

I open the door with my whole body flexed and ready for destruction. A father and son leave and I nod at them as I go to close the door.

"Hold on," Thomas' uncle says as he shuffles over. I remember this guy from my youth. He used to take us out on his boat.

"Sorry, Richard," I say as I close the door in his face. "I can't. There's a broken pipe in here."

He looks confused, but I close the door before he can say anything. I slide the lock closed and walk over to the sinks.

The guy in the gray suit is whistling as he pees at the urinal. I cross my arms, lean on the sink, and wait.

He zips up when he's done and then turns around. He looks startled when he sees me, but then quickly smiles. "I feel like I've had ten beers and pissed out twelve."

He laughs as he walks to the sink beside me and starts washing his hands.

My narrowed eyes are locked on him.

"You okay?" he asks nervously when he looks up at me.

"Give me the camera."

"Excuse me?"

I strike like a rattlesnake. In an instant, I have my hand wrapped around his throat and I'm slamming him into the full-length mirror. It shatters behind him as his eyes fly wide open.

"What the fuck?"

He can talk. I'm not squeezing hard enough.

"*Errgghh.*"

"The camera. Give. Me. The. Camera."

He quickly reaches into his pocket and pulls it out. I let

him go when I have it in my hand. He slips on the broken mirror pieces when he lands.

I start cycling through his pictures and videos as he grabs his throat and chokes.

It's all pictures of women from the wedding. Asses, tits, even a couple of up the skirt shots. My hands clench around the phone when I see the ass I would recognize anywhere covered by Violet's purple dress.

"What the fuck is this?" I show him the screen and he cringes.

"It was just… It's just a little…"

I just glare at him, knowing that nothing he can say will save him from a pounding. I think he knows it too.

"Come on, man," he says with a desperate shrug. "You know how it is to be a guy."

"This is *my* girl," I snarl when I look down at the screen. I throw it hard against the wall and it shatters into pieces.

He winces when I turn back to him. I should put this creep in a coma, but I've already ruined Thomas' wedding enough. I don't want an ambulance coming and disrupting the party as paramedics come rushing through. Let alone police coming to escort me out in handcuffs.

"You leave. Now."

He nods his head up and down like a jackhammer. His eyes are huge as I lean into him.

"If I ever see you around Violet again," I hiss. "I'm going to smash your head against that wall next time."

"You'll never see me again," he promises with a racing voice.

"Good. Now get the fuck out of here."

He rushes over to the door, unlocks it and sprints out.

I turn to the sink and spray cold water on my face, wondering what the hell is wrong with me.

Being protective is one thing. This is beyond that.

It was my possessiveness that brought me in here. I was pissed because he was looking at what was *mine*.

I look into the mirror at my pale face. The need is written all over it.

I touched her pussy but I still haven't been inside it. I've marked it, but I haven't claimed it.

The need to do so burns within me.

I'll have to get her alone and breed her quickly.

Richard walks in and frowns as he looks at the broken mirror. "I thought you said there was a broken pipe, not a broken mirror."

"And I thought I told you to stay the fuck outside."

He jerks his head back in shock and I quickly apologize for snapping.

This girl is unraveling me.

I'm falling apart.

I turn back to the sink and splash some more cold water on my face.

"Keep it together, Ash," I whisper to the reflection in the mirror. "Or, you're going to ruin everything."

CHAPTER SEVEN

Violet

MY TIPSY AUNT RUNS OVER AND STARTS DANCING WITH ME AS the DJ plays Elvis' *Hound Dog.* The crowd starts pouring onto the dance floor now that the father-daughter dance is done.

I shake my hips and smile at my aunt as my family comes dancing around us, but I'm not really into it. My focus is not here.

I'm the daughter of the groom and it's my job to help get the party started, so I stay on the dance floor, but my eyes don't. I'm looking everywhere for him.

My stomach twists with impatience and need when I can't find him. His seat is empty. He's not at the bar.

I can still feel his hand between my legs and I start to get all heated up again when I remember how good that orgasm felt. I need another. I need more.

Two songs later, I see him walking out of the bathroom. His tie is off and the top few buttons of his white shirt are open. I swallow hard when I see the tip of his chest tattoo peeking out.

I remember the summer when he got it. I was twelve and my parents had rented a cottage on a lake. Ashton came up for the day, rumbling in on his motorcycle. When he pulled off his shirt, I still remember staring at his big tattooed arms with the sexy ink sprawled across his massive chest. I was only twelve, but the sight still got me all tingly. Now, I'm full-on throbbing.

He stops at the edge of the dance floor and his eyes find me immediately. They lock on me and my dancing slowly stops until I'm standing still and staring back with my heart pounding and my breath caught somewhere near my hard nipples.

"I *love* this song," my tipsy aunt says as she crashes her hip into me. "You're not dancing!"

I nearly fall—these heels that Becky picked are ridiculous —but I manage to regain my balance without having to take my eyes off him.

"Come," he mouthes as he motions for me to follow him.

My eyes widen and I can feel my cheeks getting hot as he walks away. What does he have planned? Where is he planning to do it?

My aunt grabs me as she stumbles on her drunken feet. "I'm going to the bathroom," I tell her, but she's already dancing away as she sings at the top of her lungs. Maybe tipsy wasn't the right word. She's sloshed.

My whole body is tingling as I duck around the dancing guests. My eyes are on Ashton's muscular back as he heads toward the kitchen.

I take one step onto the regular floor and Marvin, a young guy who works at my dad's office, plows into me. He nearly knocks me down on his rush to get out. He looks panicked and his gray suit is all disheveled.

"Are you okay, Marvin?" I ask when his wide frantic eyes dart to mine. "Are you leaving already?"

"Yeah," he says with his voice racing. "I gotta... It's a..." He gulps, turns to the exit, and then rushes out without saying another word.

That was strange. I hope everything is okay.

I let out a deep exhale and then hurry over to where I last saw Ashton. He had turned the corner to where the entrance of the kitchen is.

As soon as I turn the corner, out of sight of the guests, he grabs my wrist and pulls me through the double doors.

It's intensely bright in the staff area and I squint as he holds me in the little area before the main kitchen. The cooks are cleaning up after the dinner is finished and they keep shooting us confused glances.

The waiters and waitresses are preparing the coffee in their little section and they keep looking at us too.

Ashton is only staring at me. It's like they're not even there. It's as if no one exists in his world but me.

"I want you to come to London with me."

My mouth drops open, but no words come out.

I shake my head, wondering if I heard him correctly.

"What?"

He presses his lips against mine and devours my mouth. I melt into the kiss and his strong hands are the only thing holding me up. *Oh shit...* I love it when he does that.

Little whimpers start rolling out of my throat when I feel his hands starting to creep up my ribs. I press my chest up and arch my back, wanting to feel his hot mouth on my aching nipples once again.

The doors burst open and he pulls his mouth away. I let out a whining moan as a waitress shuffles in. She's rolling her eyes and scratching her stomach. "I need a fucking cigarette so goddamn—"

Her mouth shuts and she winces when she sees us. The

professionalism she was showing with the guests is suddenly back and she gives me a quick smile before hurrying away.

"Come here." Ashton grabs my wrist and pulls me past the kitchen. The cooks are watching curiously, but they don't say a thing. Maybe they know my father is paying a fortune for this wedding and none of them want to tell the daughter of the groom that she can't be back here.

I slip on the greasy floor, but Ashton catches me. His hand is wrapped around me and it doesn't leave my hip as he pulls me down the hallway into the storage closet.

I'm surrounded by huge cans, bags of rice and beans, and lots of jars full of all sorts of non-perishables. There's one bare lightbulb hanging from the ceiling and it starts swinging back and forth after Ashton slams the door shut. He grabs the huge rack full of cans and grunts as he pulls it in front of the door, locking us in.

I'm standing in the middle of the small storage room with my hands clasped tightly in front of me. My heart is hammering against my ribs as I watch him.

Normally, this is probably the least sexy place in the hotel, but right now it feels incredibly erotic. The hot air is charged with heat and the way he's frantically locking us in is sending my pussy into a deep throb.

He turns around and I hold his heated gaze.

"Watching you move those curves on the dance floor was making me so fucking hard."

My pussy gets wetter as his hungry eyes roam all over my curves. He never takes his eyes off me as he slides his jacket off and hangs it on the rack. I swallow hard when his hands go to his belt and he starts unbuckling.

"Let me show you how fucking hard you make me." My eyes are locked on the outline of his hard cock that's visible in his pants. I've never seen a dick up close before and my heart pounds in anticipation.

He pulls it out and my mouth begins to water. Holy fuck. His cock is *huge*.

It's thick and beautiful with veins snaking up the long shaft.

A little moan falls out of my parted lips when I picture how it would feel to drag my tongue along those pulsing veins.

"Come here, Violet."

I move forward like I'm his sex slave. His commands touch something deep inside me and it's not even a question whether I should obey him or not. I just do.

"Wrap your hand around my cock. Feel how fucking hard you make me."

The sight of his hardness up close sends jolts of heat rushing straight to my core. I lick my lips as I reach down with my tingling hands.

Oh fuck.

He's as hard as a rock. My tiny hands look so small wrapped around his big shaft.

I'm not sure what to do. I've never done anything even close to this before.

"Stroke it," he commands in a dominant voice.

I swallow hard and start moving my hand up and down his cock. I'm not sure if I'm doing it right, but he seems to be liking it. His breathing is getting harder and that massive chest is heaving up and down as he grunts under his breath.

He's so big. Not just his dick, but everything. He towers over me and I feel so small and vulnerable next to him. It just turns me on even more.

"Fuck, Violet. Your soft hands feel so good on my cock. Do you like touching it?"

"Yes," I moan as I run my hand over his thick head. The skin is velvety soft up there.

"Squeeze it harder."

I tighten my grip on his shaft and his grunts start coming out deeper as I stroke him harder and faster.

A few drops of cum spill out of the tiny slit in the tip as my hand makes its way back up. My pussy is aching as I run my palm over the sticky cum and slide it back down over his cock.

He moans hard as I coat his thick veined shaft with his own cum. My palm slides easier now and I start jerking him off faster.

"My dick has been rock hard since I saw you walking down that aisle in your sexy purple dress. I wanted to rush down there, rip it off, and fuck you in front of everyone."

I feel his hot breath on my tingling skin as he talks. The excited rush of adrenaline coursing through me builds with every second that I'm touching this older man's hard cock.

"Would you have liked that? To get fucked hard by this dick?"

"Yes," I moan.

"Fuck, I can't wait to be inside you. I couldn't fucking stop smelling your ripe pussy on my fingers after I touched you outside. Tell me, sweet girl. Are you wet for me?"

"*Yes*. I'm so fucking wet."

"Keep stroking that cock."

He reaches up and cups my cheeks with his big hands. He slowly brings his mouth forward and the feeling of his hot breath on my lips mixed with the anticipation of his kiss is so intense that my legs start to go weak.

My body forgets how to breathe and I think I might pass out.

His lips come down on mine and he thrusts his tongue into my mouth, claiming every inch of it. I'm still stroking his cock with a soft rhythm, hoping he's enjoying it. At least I am.

His strong hands slide up into my hair and my perfectly styled bun becomes a perfectly hot mess. Strands of hair fall down everywhere, but I don't care. As long as his hot tongue is sliding against mine like this, everything in the world will be okay.

I moan into his mouth as his hands slide down my neck. I love the vulnerable feeling of his powerful hands on my throat like he could just choke me to sleep if he wanted to. It causes the deep throbbing between my legs to throb a little deeper. My clit is *aching* with need.

His hands slide down my shoulders and they take my straps along the way. He tugs my dress down as his hands slide over the goosebumps on my arms. My dress peels down my big breasts and my nipples harden with impatience.

He grabs my bra and yanks it down with one hard tug. My breasts spill free and he pulls his mouth away to lean back and look at them.

My lips are parted and I'm breathing heavily as he stares at my naked tits. His eyes are full of lust and desire as he stares down at them. The air in the hot room seems to charge all around us with every long second that passes. My body is stirring with excitement at being so exposed for my dad's best friend.

"I can't believe how beautiful you are. These tits are pure perfection. Everything about you is perfect."

"But I'm not like the other girls." The words just come spilling out of my mouth on their own. "I'm thick with curves."

He grabs my thick hips with a firm grip and bites his bottom lip as he comes closer. "Your body is *perfect*. You're feeling how fucking hard these gorgeous curves make me. My dick has been lusting for you all damn day."

He is so hard. No one has ever looked at me like this before. If Ashton likes my thick curves then I'm happy I have them. I only want to please him.

"It's time to test these curves out," he says as his hands cup my breasts. He runs his thumbs over my tingling nipples making them even harder.

"So pink," he says as he starts kissing them. "Tell me, is your pussy as pink?"

I just drop my head back and moan as he sucks on my right nipple. He rolls his tongue around the pink nub and then drags it over my hot skin. I'm moaning and stroking and arching my back as he loves one breast than the other. His tongue feels so good on me, but I want to feel it somewhere else.

"Let's see how pink this young pussy is," he says as his hands slide down my hips. I'm so wet and ready for him.

"This pussy is going to belong to me now. I put dibs on it when I made you cum on my hand earlier, but now I'm going to claim it. I'm taking it bare, Violet. No condom this time. Are you on the pill?"

I shake my head as he pulls up my dress. His rough hands slide under the soft material and I shift my legs to open them as his scratchy palms slide up my bare thighs.

"I haven't had a need to," I tell him in gasps and moans. I want him to know that I saved myself for him. I want him to know that he's always been the only one for me. "I'm a virgin."

His cock pulses in my hand when I say the V-word.

"You waited?"

"For you. I always wanted it to be you."

His hard face softens as he looks down at me. "I won't make you wait any longer."

I gasp as his hands grab my panties. He drops to his knees and I have to let go of his cock as he starts pulling them down.

My whole body is smoldering with the thrilling feeling of an older man pulling down my wet underwear.

The purple dress falls back down as he slides my panties past my knees. He guides my feet out of them one at a time and then shakes his head as he looks at them with a hungry look. "They're soaked through. How juicy is that virgin pussy?"

I swallow hard as he starts pulling my dress up to find out. My chest tightens when it comes up to my waist. His face is right in front of my bare cunt. I've never been exposed like this before and it's getting me so turned on that I forget how to breathe.

"Hold this," he says as he hands me the bottom of my dress. I hold the soft material as he leans back to look me over. My tits are out and my wet pussy is showing. He starts stroking his cock as he admires every inch of me.

"If I knew this was waiting for me back here, I would have left London ages ago."

"You're here now. That's all that matters."

"And I'm not leaving you this time. You're coming back to London with me."

I nod my head up and down. I'd go anywhere with him.

He puts his hand on my stomach and gently pushes me back. "Lie down."

There's a pile of huge rice bags behind me and I lie down on it.

Ashton's dark eyes are locked on my pussy as he comes forward. My eyes widen and my lips part as his head goes straight for it.

He grabs a knee in each hand and wrenches my legs apart so that I'm spread wide in front of him.

My little pink pussy is throbbing as he stares at it. I want to touch myself so badly, but I don't dare move. I'd rather wait and see what this man has in store for me.

"You're *dripping* with juices." His body is all tight and his hand starts moving even harder and faster up and down his hard cock. "I've never seen a pinker, riper pussy in all of my life. It's *begging* me to breed it and I won't say no. After I get a taste, I'm going to fuck this teenage cunt with my raw cock and give it what it wants."

My back is already arched. I'm gripping onto the rough burlap sacks as he leans in and I feel his hot breath tickling my lips. His tongue hits my folds and I let out a loud cry.

He doesn't let up. He doesn't go easy. The fucker *devours* me.

I feel his tongue *every-fucking-where*. Through my folds. Swirling around my opening. Firm and hard as it drags across my clit. All the while his strong hands are holding my legs and spreading them wide open.

I moan when I look down and see his salt and pepper hair and big broad shoulders between my legs. Seeing Ashton kneeling down there where I've always wanted him to be is almost better than the feeling of his tongue exploring my pussy.

My body shudders when he wraps his lips around my clit and grazes it with his teeth. "Oh, Ashton," I moan as I dig my fingernails into the rough burlap sacks.

We're in the storage room of a banquet hall. We're at my father's *wedding!* My whole family is outside probably wondering where I am. There are cooks and servers that can hear me moaning and crying out loud. This is so wrong. But I'm so consumed with lust that I don't even care.

Ashton's made me lose my mind.

All that's left is *need*.

His thick fingers slide inside me and I grip onto the sack of rice under me to root myself so I don't fall off the earth and spiral into the abyss.

Everything feels so good. So *right*.

I'm rolling my hips on his mouth as he plays with my clit. He grabs my ass and pulls me into him, trying to get as much of my young cunt into his mouth as he can.

My pussy starts to contract and I brace myself. I know what's coming. I felt it outside on his hand, but it's going to be even harder on his mouth. His tongue is relentless. He's desperate to get me off.

Little grunts and groans of approval keep rumbling out of him and they tickle my pussy as he eats me out.

I move my hand into his hair and grip it as I roll my hips against his face. I'm so fucking close. I can feel it coming like an unstoppable force. My hips and his tongue find a smooth steady rhythm and I ride it long enough for my orgasm to grip me. It tightens every cell in my body until I'm ready to scream and then it *releases*.

"*Fuuccckkk.*" I throw my head back and cry out as the heated waves come crashing down on me, sending me spiraling under the weight of it.

I'm crying out. Legs shaking. Head back. Teary-eyed. Ashton keeps licking me even though I'm squeezing his ears as hard as I can with my thighs. I'm pulling his hair and gasping as he slides his fingers out of my wet hole and replaces them with his tongue.

When the white spots finally leave my vision and I collapse onto his broad shoulders, I'm breathing heavily and wondering what the fuck just happened.

Ashton rises to his knees and looks at me with the hardest, sexiest stare I've ever seen. His mouth and chin are slick with my desire and I watch with my heart pounding as he wipes it off with his hand and then licks his palm.

"Fuck, you taste sweet. That pussy is juicier than a ripe peach."

I gulp as he starts stroking his hard cock once again. If his fingers felt that thick inside of me, I'm afraid to find out what his huge dick is going to feel like.

"Tell me you want it. Tell me you want me to fuck you with this big cock."

My eyes are wide and fixated on it. His hand is busy stroking it up and down. Every stroke brings another drop of cum oozing out. He's ready to unload all of that into my pussy, and I'm ready to let him.

"I want it."

"Want what?"

"Your big *cock*. I want you to fuck my pussy with it."

He grins as he squeezes his shaft and brings it toward me. I gasp when I feel his thick head parting my folds. His cum is on me now. He's marked me. It's his.

My whole body tightens and I squeeze the sacks of rice as he presses his swollen head to my tight little hole. "*Oh, shit,*" I hiss as he starts to press it inside.

It feels so *big*. He makes me feel so tiny.

"This pussy is tighter than I thought," he groans as he slowly, agonizingly pushes the tip inside. He barely gets half the head in when there's a pounding on the door.

Ashton whips his head around, taking his beautiful cock with him. I gasp at the loss. I barely had any of him inside me, but I want it back. I need it in me.

The pounding continues. Harder.

"*Open up!*"

The handle is jiggling and the rack starts jerking around as the guy tries to open the door.

"*You're not allowed in there!*"

"Shit," Ashton curses as he jumps to his feet. "Put your clothes on. I don't want to have to kill this guy if he comes in here and sees you like this."

I quickly get to my feet, but my legs are all wobbly and it catches me off guard. I grab onto the wall before I fall over.

Ashton pulls up his pants and a feeling of disappointment fills me when he puts his cock away. I quickly find my panties and put them on even though they're soaking wet. I tuck my breasts back in my dress as Ashton puts on his jacket.

We look like a mess. My hair looks like I drove through a tornado while sticking my head out of the sunroof and I'm sure my makeup is just as bad. Ashton's hair is sticking up in places like he just woke up from a deep sleep on the couch.

"*This is the manager! Open the door!*"

"Hold on," Ashton growls.

He drags the metal rack away from the door and yanks it open. The manager is standing in the hall, red-faced and looking pissed. Until he sees the size of Ashton and the look on his face.

The man cowers before my eyes and drops his submissive gaze to the floor. "Sorry, sir. You can't be in here."

Ashton grabs my wrist, grunts at the guy, and pulls me out of there.

I have to jog to keep up with him as he pulls me back into the hall where the party is going strong. He heads right for the door that I know leads up to his hotel room, but the bride, who is now my new stepmother, blocks our way.

"Violet," she says as she grabs my other arm. "It's time for the bouquet toss. I waited for you since it's the only chance you'll have to get married."

Her vile eyes suddenly dart over and she sees Ashton's hand wrapped around my wrist. A cruel smile creeps across her mouth and I shudder.

Shit.

Busted.

CHAPTER EIGHT

Violet

I END UP CATCHING THE BOUQUET. PROBABLY BECAUSE BECKY whips it right at me.

It hits me in the chest and I wrap my hands around, hoping the old superstition is true. I want to be the next girl to be married and I know to who.

Ashton is watching me from the edge of the dance floor. I pulled my hair down since it was a big mess and he can't seem to take his eyes off it.

Becky has a wicked grin on her face as she struts over. She's all smiles and nice words to the crowd, but once she leans in close, it's all mean words and vile.

"Sadly, Violet, I don't even think that fate would be able to get you a man." She's shaking her head and looking at me with pity.

My jaw is clenched as I glare back at her. Hate is radiating off me.

"I can get a man." *I already have one.*

She tilts her head and shakes it like I'm the most naive girl in the world.

"I'm sure you can get an old man drunk enough to use you as a cum dumpster for one night. But try to keep him around in the morning and you'll find out just how truly interested he is in you. I think you'll be *very* disappointed."

"You're a real bitch, Becky."

I want to lay this cunt out with a punch to the jaw, but I wouldn't do that to my dad.

Her cruel green eyes narrow on me. "You think I've been a bitch? You haven't seen *anything*. Watch this shit."

My stomach drops as she charges away. She heads straight for my father who is speaking with two of his managers that work for him. They're beside the five-layered cake with the happy little plastic couple on top.

I race after her as dread creeps through me.

"Thomas!" she snaps. My father turns around and the two managers quickly leave when they see her pissed off face. Smart move. It's probably why my father promoted them.

"What?" He looks from her to me with a confused look on his face. "What happened?"

"I'm distressed," she says as she wipes the back of her forehead with her hand. I haven't seen such bad acting since my high school put on Macbeth. "I discovered your daughter doing something naughty."

He chuckles as he looks at me. "It's a wedding, Becky. She can have a couple of drinks. I don't mind."

"It's not *straws* that she's been sucking on."

No. My chest tightens. I feel dizzy.

"Your daughter has been sleeping around with Ashton!"

My body tenses as I wait for the thunder to come, but my dad just starts laughing. Hard. Becky looks furious as it turns into a deep belly laugh.

"It's true," she snaps as she crosses her arms. "I saw them together."

"Don't be ridiculous," he says as he wipes the tears from his eyes. "Ashton got here right before the wedding."

"Ask her."

They both turn to me and my face gives it all away.

"You?" he says as his face turns pale. "And Ashton…"

He charges away and I hurry to follow him, but Becky grabs me and yanks me back. She's got a triumphant look on her face.

"I guess daddy's little girl is not so perfect. He's *my* daddy now."

I'm done playing nice with this cunt. I grab the top layer of the cake and ram it into her face.

I grind it hard against her before letting it go.

And then I leave.

CHAPTER NINE

Ashton

Now I know how all those poor rugby players felt when the great Thomas the Tank came charging at them. His face is red. His nostrils are flaring. He's ready to break something and he's got his eyes on me.

My best friend looks *pissed*.

He grabs my collar and doesn't stop moving until we're outside.

The last thing I want to do is fight with my oldest friend, especially at his wedding.

Apparently, he doesn't feel the same way.

He grabs me by the lapel and slams my back into the brick wall. I grunt as the back of my head bounces off the brick.

"What did you do?" he screams into my face.

A few people follow us out and are watching with shocked looks on their faces. "Get the fuck back inside!" he shouts and they all scatter like roaches.

"You, and my… Violet?"

"I love her, Thomas."

He punches me hard in the stomach. I bend over with a grunt.

Luckily, I don't miss too many ab days or that big cinderblock fist would have gone right through to my spine.

"I fucking love her."

He cocks his fist back and I wince when I see him clenching his jaw.

"Hit me if you want, but it's not going to change a damn thing."

He slams his fist into my cheek and I see stars. My leg gives out and I drop to a knee.

I think I could take him. I've been hitting the gym over the years, while he's been hitting the donuts, but I'm not going to fight back. Not with him.

I'd kill for Violet, but I'd also take a beating for her.

Water fills my eyes as pain shoots through my brain like bolts of lightning. He grabs my collar and yanks me up. Before I know it, his big hands are pinning me against the brick wall again.

"She's my fucking daughter!" he screams into my face. His hot breath and spit slam into my bruised cheek. "She's eighteen-years-old!"

He hits me again, and again, and again.

Two to the stomach, then one to my nose.

I drop down, coughing and bleeding from my nostrils. I feel the warmth of it trickling onto my lips as the taste of copper fills my mouth.

His chest is heaving and his big fist is cocked back, ready to dish out more.

"You know me better than anyone, Thomas," I say between coughs. "When have I ever used a girl? You know me. I don't sleep around. I haven't had sex in four years."

The mention of sex gets me another punch to the temple

and it sends the world spinning for a few seconds. Poor choice of words. I guess I deserved that one.

"I'd never touch your daughter unless it was true love. You know that."

He staring at me with fire in his eyes as he squeezes his fist. "She's my little girl. She's so pure and innocent, and you want to take that from her."

I *will* take that from her. A million beatings can't stop that.

"I love her, Thomas. We're going to be together. You can fight it, but it's going to happen."

He cocks his fist back and I close my eyes and wince, but it never comes.

"Get the fuck out of here," he says when I open my eyes. "You're dead to me."

I walk into my hotel room feeling like shit. My eye is starting to swell up and my lip is all busted open. But that's not what's bothering me.

I fucked things up with Thomas.

He'll probably never speak to me again. He'll probably want to kill me when he finds out that I'm bringing his daughter to London.

And I am.

Even after that beating, I'm taking her.

There's no way I can let that girl go. I've tasted that sweet nectar she's got between those thick legs and nothing—even the threat of Thomas the Tank hunting me down—is going to stop me.

I unbutton my ripped shirt and pull it off my body. I'm all bruised up.

Where the fuck is she?

It's all I can think about. It's making me all prickly inside that I don't know where she is. I don't know who she's talking to. Who's looking at her.

"*Fuck.*" I slam my fist into the bed as my pulse starts racing.

I want her *here. Now.*

I need to keep track of her better than this. My mind goes to fucked up places. Locking a tracking device on her ankle. Tying her to the bed.

"I can't stay here," I mutter as I grab my shirt. I need to find her. I need to know where she is.

I rush to the door and open it, but I jump back with a gasp when I nearly run her over. She's standing in the doorway with tears in her eyes.

The anger just rushes out of me as I take her in my arms and pull her into the room. She melts against my bare chest and sobs. Her wet tears streak my hot skin and it makes my cock rock hard.

I just hold her tight and let her cry. I'll be the shoulder for her to cry on. I'll be her rock. I'll be whatever she needs.

My nose goes to her hair and I inhale long and deep, sucking in the delicious vanilla scent of her shampoo. It fills my bruised nose and makes me lightheaded.

"Oh my god," she says when she sees a bruise on my ribs. It's already turning blue. Thomas the Tank didn't get that nickname for nothing.

She steps back and gasps when she looks at my face.

"Did my father do this?" she asks as she gently runs her soft hand over my face. Her thumb glides over my split lip and I kiss it.

"It's okay," I say as I pull her back into my arms. "I'm a tough old bastard."

"You're not that old," she says with a soft smile. Her hand goes to my swollen eye that will be black as fuck tomorrow.

I'm too old for her according to everyone out there, but I

don't give a fuck. This is *our* life. Not there's. It doesn't matter what they think.

"I came here to tell you that I'm coming."

My heart feels so light that I think it might float out of my chest. I just grip her arms, unable to say anything.

"To London. I want to go to London with you."

There are no words to say. She's made me the happiest man in the world. I pull her forward and kiss her with all of the love and passion that she's built up inside me.

"We're going to be so happy, Violet," I say when we finally pull away. "I'm going to treat you right. I promise."

"I know." Her eyes drop to my tattooed chest and she licks my taste off of her lips. She traces her fingertips over my ink and her touch is so soft that it tickles my chest. "I always wanted to touch you here. Ever since I was a little girl. I dreamed about these tattoos."

"You're not a little girl anymore." My hands start moving to her big tits and she lets out a little moan. "It's time to make you into a woman. It's time to take away that innocence."

She looks into my eyes with the sexiest look and nods her head up and down.

I don't want to know what I would have done if she came here to tell me she was staying. All I know is that I would have probably ended up in jail.

I reach down and slide my hand behind her legs and scoop her up in my arms. She's still tracing my tattoos over my round shoulder as I hold her to my chest and carry her to the bed.

My dick is aching with her in my arms. I don't understand what she's done to me, but I don't try to figure it out. Some things are beyond the mind. This goes right to our souls. They seem to be locked on each other at a molecular level.

Our souls need each other. They're making our lives miserable and tearing us to pieces when they're apart, but when they're together… it's pure bliss.

I lower her onto the bed and stand back just to admire her for a moment before I ravage her.

Her brown hair is splayed all around her head and she's looking up at me with sexy blue fuck me eyes. She slowly spreads her legs open and pulls her dress up, showing me her wet panties.

"You want my cock back, don't you baby girl?"

She bites her bottom lip and starts rolling her thick hips. She fucking wants it.

"This time I won't stop at the tip. This time I'm sliding *all* the way inside with my raw cock and I'm going to fuck that pussy right."

A groan slips out of my mouth when I see her hand slide down into her underwear. She starts playing with her cunt and a rage hits me that I'm missing it. I grab her panties and rip them off her, tearing the wet fabric that's been soaked all night.

Now I can watch her as she slides her fingers up and down her wet slit. She dips one into her virgin hole and I groan when I remember how fucking tight it was. A rush of juices squirts out and my mouth waters.

I can't move. I want to go to her, but my feet are glued to the floor as I stand here staring, completely transfixed. The sweet scent of her honey fills the room and my heart starts hammering in my chest.

When she pulls her wet fingers away and starts sucking on them, I finally snap out of it.

"Take that dress off. Take *everything* off. Now."

She moans and then sits up to unzip the back of her dress. My hands are on my belt, fumbling as I try to undo my buckle in record time. I slide it out and then pull down my pants and boxer briefs.

My curvy girl is wiggling out of her dress by the time I walk over with my hard dick in my hand.

"Come here, girl," I say as I sit on the bed with my back

against the pillows. "I want to see these big tits bouncing up and down as you ride my dick."

She puts a hand on my shoulder and straddles me. *Oh fuck.* The sight of her spread pussy over my cock is making my heart hurt. She's so fucking perfect.

I grab her thick waist as she reaches down and grips my shaft. She drags the tip of my dick along her slit a couple of times before pressing it up against her virgin hole.

She's even tighter than I remember. I hiss in a breath when she drops her hips down onto the head of my cock. It goes in slowly, painfully, she's so fucking tight. My head is pressed back against the headboard and I'm breathing heavily as I watch her descending on my cock. A flood of warm juices trickles out of her and rolls down my shaft. I moan when I feel it coating my balls.

Everything is turning me on. Knowing I'm the first to slide into this ripe cunt. Watching her take me raw and unprotected. Her big tits with her firm little hard nipples in my face. Knowing that she'll be carrying my child soon. It's all too much.

Her pussy swallows my entire head and then slides down my shaft until she gasps and I feel a bit of resistance.

"Take a deep breath, Violet." Her body is so tight and her pussy is all clenched up on my cock. I start to rub her wet clit to help ease some of the squeezing and loosen her up before I bust through her cherry.

"Just do it," she moans as she closes her eyes. I thrust up and pop through it, taking her innocence away forever. Her tight jaw melts into a moan and her lips fall open as I slide all the way in. The heat is unreal. It's so warm and tight and wet. I want to keep my cock in here forever.

"Oh, Ashton," she moans with a wince on her face. "You're *so* big. Your cock is *huge*."

I start playing with her tits, gripping them with my hands as I kiss a wet trail around her hard pink nipples. This seems to distract her and she moans with pleasure as her cunt gets used to my size.

Eventually, she starts to rock her hips and her wet silky walls release some of the insanely tight grip on me.

"This cunt is definitely coming back with me to London. And it's never leaving."

"I would never leave you," she moans as she begins slowly rising up and down, testing her ripe pussy out.

"I would never let you. You'll be pregnant by the time the wheels hit the runway in the UK and that'll mean you can never go. Your fresh womb is mine now." I slide my hands over her tits and give them a squeeze. "These are mine. This pussy is mine. All of you is mine."

She drops her head back and closes her eyes as she starts riding me. "I've always been yours, Ashton. I'm so happy you finally realize it."

My curvy girl is completely relaxed now and riding my length up and down. Every drop of her hips sends a little bit of juices squirting onto my balls. She's so ripe and fertile. It's only going to take this one time to get her pregnant.

One time to breed her. The next thousand until she gives birth will just be for fun. Then I'll breed this teenage pussy again and again and again.

She slides her cunt down on me and grinds her clit hard against the base of my cock. The sexy little moans that keep coming out of her mouth are making me so hard. I love watching her enjoying herself on my dick.

I can tell she's close to her climax when her moans turn into whimpers and her hips start moving faster. She presses her palms on my abs and digs her fingernails into them as she rides me energetically.

"Yes," she moans as she slams her pussy down on my cock. "Your dick feels so *fucking* good."

I grab her soft ass cheeks and start thrusting up as she comes down. We slam into each other with every thrust until her legs start jerking around and she's crying out loud. Her orgasm hits her *hard*. She screams out in agony or bliss or surprise—or probably all three. Her fingernails drag down my bruised skin as the orgasm sears through her like a wildfire.

Her pussy clenches on me and I can't breathe, it's so tight. My obsession reaches a boiling point and there's only one thought in my head: to breed her now.

I grab her and twist her until she's on her back and I'm on top. I'm fucking her hard and erratic. Pumping my hips with frenzied deep thrusts as fast as I can. This is no sweet loving making. No romance. This is hardcore fucking with one end goal—to bathe her teenage womb in my cum.

Her legs are up and her head is back. She's screaming out as I slam my cock into her one hard thrust after another. The obsession has taken over. I've lost my cool.

I *need* to breed her. I need it *now*.

She cums on my cock again and her warm juices flow out between us. I don't stop. I don't even slow down to give her a break. I just keep fucking her relentlessly. Savagely. Like a fucking animal.

Her tight little pussy cums again or maybe it's the same one that's lasting forever. I don't know. I can't think. There's only one word flashing in my head over and over again. *Breed. Breed. Breed.*

I wrap my hand around her neck and give her a little squeeze to know that I'm in charge. She opens her mouth and gasps, but her eyes are alive with excitement. She likes it.

Finally, it comes rushing forward. It's been building all day. My balls have been aching with all of the cum this girl has made me create and now it's going to burst out into her fresh cunt.

I thrust hard once, twice, and then I root in deep and release. I squeeze her neck and push my cock all the way inside her as I cum hard. My load shoots out of me into her teenage pussy so hard that I feel lightheaded instantly. It's the best orgasm of my life. It's the most important orgasm of my life.

My girl cums too and this time I can tell for sure. Her back arches and she's thrashing around under me as I fill her silky tunnel with my seed.

She's breathing heavily and gasping for air as I release the grip on her throat. "That was incredible," she gasps as the color comes back to her face. "I can't even…" The words fall out of her mouth and she just stares up at me in awe.

I kiss her hard on the lips and taste her once more. I can't get enough of this girl.

She's coming home with me.

I still can't believe it.

"Why are you smiling?" she asks as her lips curl up into her own smile.

"You're coming to London with me. It makes me happy."

She leans up and kisses me on the lips.

"You won't be saying that when you hear my British accent."

I laugh.

As soon as we're done here, I'm bringing her to the airport and we're getting on the first airplane back.

We both start rocking our hips and my cock hardens inside of her.

As soon as we're done here…

But I'm not finished yet.

CHAPTER TEN

Violet

Four weeks later…

"WHERE IS IT?" I MUTTER.

I'm searching through Ashton's huge fridge when I feel his hands on me. He spins me around, pushes me up against the cold shelves, and kisses me hard.

"*Mmmmm,*" I moan as his tongue slides against mine.

He pulls away but his firm grip remains on my waist as he looks down at me with an unforgiving look. "You're taking too long."

"I was gone for thirty seconds!"

"That's too long."

I laugh as he pushes my hair away and starts kissing my neck. His cock pushes up against my stomach and I moan when I feel how hard he is.

This guy doesn't act his age. We just had about an hour of sex and he's ready for more. The man is insatiable. I love it.

"I was just looking for some orange juice. I'm so thirsty!"

I'm wearing nothing but his t-shirt that goes down to my legs. He's wearing nothing but a smile on his face.

It's about eight in the morning on a Saturday and so far, the weekend is looking good.

He reaches behind me and grabs the carton of OJ. "Drink up," he says as he shoves it into my hand. My pussy starts tingling when I feel his hands grabbing my shirt and pulling it up my legs. Is this really happening *again?*

"All of the liquids in your body are going straight to this sweet juicy cunt," he says as he drops to his knees in front of me. He's licking his lips and looking at my pussy like he's just found his breakfast.

"I wonder who's fault that is…" I take a sip of the cold orange juice straight from the carton and it's the best thing I've ever tasted.

Ashton doesn't even let me finish before he lifts me up and spreads my legs. Orange juice spills on my shirt as I grab a hold of the shelves in the fridge. He places my ass onto the cold plastic and wastes no time diving right in.

Fuck, this guy knows how to lick a pussy. He's all over me and I'm holding onto the clear fiberglass shelves for dear life. My left foot is resting on a jar of pickles in the door and my right foot is draped over his shoulder as his greedy hot tongue ravages me.

His hand reaches up and grabs my loose breast over my shirt. He squeezes it and the feeling of his old scratchy shirt on my nipples makes them hard and pointy.

But it's his tongue that has all of my attention. It's swirling through my wet folds and dipping into my tight hole. He flicks it on my clit and then does it all over again, groaning and muttering in satisfaction like he can't get enough of it.

The cool air from the fridge feels so good on my hot skin. We're going to have to do it in this position more often.

When I feel his hard fingers on the soft flesh of my inner thighs, lifting them up, spreading them apart, it starts to set me off. I feel another orgasm coming and it's coming on harder than the two he just gave me in the bedroom.

I woke up like this: with his head between my legs and his tongue on my pussy. I'm having breakfast like this: with his head between my legs and his tongue on my pussy. And I'll probably have my shower like this: with his head between my legs and his tongue on my pussy.

I *love* London.

When the orgasm hits, it fucking hits. It's like an earthquake rocks my core. First, my legs start shaking and then my back starts convulsing. I grab onto something, anything for support and I end up knocking over a carton of Almond milk and a bowl of strawberries. They bounce off Ashton's flexed back and shoulders, but he doesn't stop devouring me.

My mouth is open and I'm screaming out his name as my shaking foot kicks a jar of salad dressing down. It shatters on the floor, and still, he doesn't stop. He pushes my legs out farther apart and digs his tongue in deeper as I knock over a bottle of maple syrup, which lands in the salad dressing.

Maybe the fridge wasn't such a great idea.

He stands up between my legs when the worst of my orgasm is done. But *he's* not done. He's just getting started.

I'm panting and gasping as little tremors come rippling through my body.

He grabs his hard cock and slides it up my slit.

More tremors. More warm shivers. More gasping.

I love London. Hail the Queen!

He presses his thick tip to my hole and pushes it inside slowly, perfectly, heavenly, beautifully. "Oh shit," I whine as he slowly slides it all the way inside. He grabs the back of my neck and pulls me forward until my forehead is resting on his big tattooed chest. I can hear his heart hammering in there and I smile, knowing it's beating for me.

His muscular hips slide back out and then right before he's about to leave me, he slides back in.

Could life be better?

Heaven is going to feel like waiting inside a doctor's office compared to my time here with him. How could it compare? It can't.

His dick stretches me. Fills me. Kills me. My body is on fire as he stuffs me. I roll my hips, grinding my aching clit onto the base of his perfect cock.

He reaches past my head and grabs the carton of orange juice. He's still all the way inside me as he takes a long gulp. I watch with a grin on my face as it leaks out the side of his mouth and trickles onto his chest and down his abs. He's the sexiest thing ever created. That I'm sure of.

He gasps when he's done and kisses me long and hard with a mouth that's all cold and citrusy.

"Tastes like breakfast," I say with a lick of my lips when he pulls away. He hands me the carton and I take my own long sip. It's a shock of cold liquid pouring through my heated body. Just what I needed.

He takes it from my hand when his impatience boils over and puts it back on the shelf beside my head. Then the fucking continues.

More food doesn't make it. The guacamole. Dijon mustard. A carton of eggs. They all die for the cause.

I'll mourn them later. Right now, I'm too busy screaming out my man's name as he drives in deep.

It's one hard relentless thrust after another and my greedy little pussy takes every one of them like a champ.

Ashton starts grunting a little deeper. His thrusts are a little harder. I'm practically all the way in the fridge now as he starts his big finish.

I feel another orgasm coming too. It builds and takes over,

first my fingers then my toes. It works its way in until it hits my core and everything unravels. I scream way too loud as the orgasm thunders through me like a whirlwind of heat and chaos.

Ashton thrusts in hard and grunts as he cums deep in my pussy. His whole body is flexed and tight. I run my hands all over his muscles, loving the feeling. The feeling of his hot fierce breath on my cool skin, the feeling of his taut muscles under my fingertips, and the feeling of his warm cum coating my silky walls.

After a few long moments of gasping for air and clinging onto each other, he reaches for the OJ and hands it to me.

Fridge sex. I highly recommend you try it.

About twenty minutes later, the coffee is brewing, the eggs are sizzling, and we're cleaning up the mess of sticky maple syrup, egg yolk, Almond milk, salad dressing, Dijon mustard, and guacamole on the floor when there's a knock at the door.

I quickly run to the bedroom—slipping on the guacamole as I go—and grab some clothes as the knocking continues. I put my pajamas on and grab a shirt and pants for Ashton.

"Put these on," I say as I toss them at him. The guy's buck naked at the stove while he's cooking the eggs. Normally I don't mind, but it's a bit much when we have guests.

He looks at me like I'm crazy as he catches the clothes.

"What if it's Girl Guides selling cookies? They're going to come in here and see you like that!"

"Fine," he says with a shake of his head. I wait until he's dressed and then I open the door.

The sight that's waiting for me staggers me.

It's my father.

I haven't seen or spoken to him since the night of the wedding.

My mouth drops open and I take an involuntary step back.

He gives me a sad smile. "Hi, pumpkin."

I stare at him, not knowing what to expect. "Hi, Dad."

"Can I come in?"

I step out of the way and nod.

He steps into the room and Ashton drops the spatula into the sizzling pan as he turns to him with a look of shock on his face.

"Thomas…"

"Hi, Ashton."

Everyone just stares at each other in a long awkward silence until my dad shrugs. "Is anyone going to offer me some of that fresh coffee or should I get it myself."

I shake out of my daze and realize I'm still holding the door wide open. I quickly close it and get my father a cup of coffee as he sits down at the island.

"Want some eggs?" Ashton asks him with a weary look on his face.

"Are they going to be all runny in the middle?" He looks at me with a grin. "This guy never knew how to cook a fucking egg. He used to swallow them down raw when we were in college."

"The runnier the better," Ashton says with a grin.

"Sure, give me a couple. I had a long fucking flight."

"A couple of eggs, coming up," Ashton says as he turns back to the pan. "Extra runny."

My dad laughs.

A sense of relief washes over me. I didn't realize how much it's been weighing on me until now. I hated that I wasn't on speaking terms with my father, and I hated that Ashton wasn't either. It's so nice to see them laughing together once again.

I hand him the coffee and he smiles sadly at me.

"You look good, pumpkin. You look happy."

"What are you doing here, Dad?"

He looks down at the coffee in his cup and sighs. "I'm sorry about how I reacted at the wedding."

Ashton turns and raises an eyebrow as he looks at him.

"It was sudden and unexpected. I didn't realize you two were in love. I thought you were taking advantage of her and I snapped. The scotches and wine didn't help either."

My mind is swirling with thoughts as I watch him. Does that mean he's okay with us being together?

His eyes meet mine and my whole body tenses. "You were right about Becky. I should have listened. You were always a better judge of character than I was."

"What happened?" I ask.

He sighs. "Her true colors were revealed after you threw the wedding cake in her face. She lost it and started saying the most horrible things."

"About me?"

"About you, about our guests, about me, about everything. She was furious. The next morning, I dragged her to the courthouse and we got it annulled."

A sudden giddiness fills my body as relief washes over me. I don't ever have to see that cunt again.

"I've thought about it a lot since then, and I regret so much. I rushed into it. I just wanted to be happy again like I was with your mother."

I go over to him and hug his huge body. "You will be, Dad. You'll find someone."

He places his hand over mine and squeezes it.

"But what I regret the most is how I treated you two. You guys are my two favorite people in the world. I'm legitimately happy that you found love with each other. It's a beautiful thing."

"Really?" I ask, hoping it's true.

He nods. "You have my blessing."

"Thanks, Thomas," Ashton says. "It means a lot."

My father looks at him and sighs. "I'm sorry I lost my shit and knocked you around."

"No big deal," Ashton says with a sly grin. "You hit like a little girl."

My dad laughs loud and hard. "Please. Your eyes were rolling around in that hard head of yours."

"I was looking for an open window. I thought I felt a breeze coming in and then I realized that it was your weak ass punches."

They keep going at it until we're all laughing and everything that happened is water under the bridge.

"I did bring a peace offering," my father says as he reaches for his bag. "I got you a wedding photo."

"That's okay, Dad," I say, shaking my head as he pulls out an 8x10. There's no way I'm keeping a photo of Becky in this place.

"No, you're going to like this one."

He hands me the photo and I burst out laughing. It's of the bride when she's covered in wedding cake. Big chunks of vanilla cake are stuck to her cheeks and hair. She's covered in icing. It's going over the fireplace.

The night might not have worked out for the bride and groom, but it was the best wedding I've ever been to.

I got the man I've always loved to finally love me back.

And I couldn't be happier.

EPILOGUE

Ashton

Two years later…

THE DOCTOR PUTS THE BABY IN MY ARMS AND MY WHOLE WORLD shifts when I look into his squished up little face.

My first child. My first son.

I stare at him as Violet rubs my back and looks over my shoulder.

This girl is truly amazing. She's given me everything. A purpose, happiness, and now this beautiful baby boy.

I turn around and look at her in awe. She just had a long grueling labor and her hair is all plastered to her sweaty temples. The poor girl is exhausted and her eyes are half closed, but she's smiling and trying to force herself to stay awake so she can witness this amazing moment.

Her skin is pale and she's wearing a faded blue hospital

gown, but to me, she's never looked more beautiful. I kiss her softly on the mouth and then turn back to my son.

"Fatherhood suits you," she says as she rests her chin on my shoulder and looks down at the adorable baby.

I'm glad because I'm not stopping at one.

The past nine months have been incredible and I've never found a woman sexier. Watching my young bride walk around with her rounded belly and full tits was a dream come true.

I can't wait for the doctor to give us the okay so I can breed her again.

"Are you okay?" I give her a kiss on her sweaty temple as she closes her eyes.

"Just tired."

"You're a warrior princess, you know that?"

She smiles.

"You were amazing. I'll never forget this."

"I didn't have much of a choice," she says with a soft laugh. "He was coming out whether I wanted it or not."

The two of us are now three and the love in our house is going to multiply even more.

We hear someone arguing with the nurses in the hallway and then suddenly the door bursts open.

"Sir! You can't go in there!"

It's Thomas. He's rushing in to see his new grandson. He must have jumped on a plane for London the second that Violet started having contractions.

"It's okay," Violet says with a smile. "He's the grandfather."

The nurse huffs out a breath and then walks out of the room shaking her head.

"Can I?" Thomas is staring at the baby with wide eyes. He's completely captivated.

"Here you go, gramps." I hand him the baby and I can tell

he's already totally in love. This kid is going to get spoiled rotten.

Violet's arms wrap around my ribs and she clings to me as she watches her father and her new son with tears in her eyes.

They've been closer than ever since Becky got the boot. He has a new fiancee and this time he's chosen right. She's so sweet and they look so happy together. Violet loves Laura and she can't wait for her to be her step-mother.

Before I saw Violet at the wedding, I had no family. I didn't realize how alone I'd been.

But now I'm surrounded by so much love, and it's only the beginning.

Because our little family is going to get *a lot* bigger.

One child at a time.

EPILOGUE

Violet

Six years later…

THE TURQUOISE WATER IS SO CRYSTAL CLEAR THAT YOU CAN SEE the translucent fish swimming over the white sand at the bottom of the ocean. This place is unbelievable.

"What island is this one?" I look over my shoulder at Ashton who is walking up to me. He's shirtless and with three weeks into our two month trip of touring the Greek islands on our new yacht, his dark tan is bringing his hotness up to a whole new level. I lick my lips as my eyes quickly roam over his ripped body and sexy tattoos. They've done this millions of times over the past eight years we've been together.

"This is Milos."

I stare in amazement at the stunning white rocks that jut

out of the turquoise water. It looks like we're vacationing on the moon.

"It's gorgeous."

He's not even looking. His eyes are locked on me. Typical Ashton.

"Take that top off. You're in Europe now."

"But I'm still an American at heart. I can't with the boys around."

We both look back to the stern of the yacht. Our four boys are checking the fishing lines with their Greek manny, who oddly enough is also named Manny. Maybe being a manny was what he was born to do.

"Manny!" Ashton calls to him. "Bring the boys onto the beach. We'll catch up in a few minutes."

Manny nods. He knows the deal about how Ashton needs his 'alone' time with his wife a few times a day.

"All right, boys," he says to them. "Last one to the beach is a dirty malaka."

I laugh as they all jump into the gorgeous water and start swimming. Manny pulls my youngest, Ethan, by his lifejacket.

"Bye, boys," I say as I wave to them. "I'll be there soon."

"No, you won't."

Ashton is standing over me and I start breathing heavier when I see the long hard bulge that he's got in his bathing suit.

"Now. Take off your top."

My nipples are already as hard as pebbles as I reach behind my back and take off my top. I place it next to me, but he kicks it away.

He's blocking my sun as he stares down at me with his chest heaving.

"Now the bottoms. Off."

This time I don't argue. He's got that heated look in his

eye and if I don't move fast, he'll rip them off—he's done it before.

I lay back on the bow of our yacht, completely naked.

"What about you, Captain?" I ask with my eye on his hard cock. "Am I going to see that big anchor of yours?"

"Fuck yeah, you will," he says as he starts untying his board shorts. "You're going to see it nice and close."

My mouth is already watering when it springs out. He kicks off his board shorts and grips his big dick as he steps up to me.

I watch in awe as he strokes his veined cock at my eye level. It's always overflowing with cum when I'm around. A delicious bead drops to the ground and I groan, hating to waste any of it.

I lean back on my hands and open my mouth up wide. The hot Greek sun is making things even hotter as he starts jerking off over my tongue.

Drop after drop of his salty-sweet cum drips onto my tongue and I'm moaning and arching up for more.

"Who knew that my innocent virgin wife would turn into a greedy little cum slut?" He has a grin on his face as he keeps stroking his cock and dripping more of it into my mouth. He's loving it as much as I am.

"Luckily for you, I'm only a greedy slut for your cock."

He lets out a deep groan as I reach up and slide my lips over his swollen head. I don't stop at the tip.

My pussy is aching in anticipation. This is just a little foreplay. It's ready for the main course.

His hands sink into my tangled hair as I take as much of him into my mouth as I can without choking. I don't use my hands. Just my mouth—sliding my lips up and down his thick hard shaft until we're both moaning for more.

Suddenly, he pulls his cock away from me and is dropping to his knees.

"Turn around," he orders, but he doesn't even wait for me

to move. His strong impatient hands are already turning my body in the way he wants it. I'm on my hands and knees with my bare ass in the air.

I gasp when he drags his tongue up my wet cunt in one long lap. It's sudden and hot and so fucking good.

Ashton always likes to have my taste on his lips and my scent in his nose when he takes me. He does it every time.

I push my thick hips back and moan when I feel his swollen head push up against my dripping wet hole.

We're anchored in front of this gorgeous secluded white sand beach with the sun on our bodies and the ocean breeze in our hair.

Luckily, the yacht slowly turned and our kids can't see us doing this from the shore. All I see in front of me is beautiful blue ocean as I feel him slide deep inside.

This has been an amazing trip. Not just the trip to Greece, but the whole thing. Everything with Ashton. The past eight years have been a dream.

He takes me hard and fast and I cum twice on his cock before he's done. His strong hands grip my ass cheeks and he cums hard.

I moan with a smile on my face when I feel his perfect cock pulsing. He releases his load deep inside me and I feel it start to warm me from the inside out.

It's incredible, but the best part is yet to come.

We both leap off the yacht into the cool crystal water below. It's an invigorating thrill after getting so hot and sweaty in the sweltering sun.

I pop out of the water with a huge smile on my face. Ashton is waiting for me like a sexy merman. His salt and pepper hair is slicked back and little droplets of water are racing down his beautiful face. He's so hot.

He reaches out, grabs me, and pulls me into his big arms as our huge yacht floats nearby.

"I love you, Violet," he says before kissing my lips.

I moan in content as he lets me go. He's still holding onto my arm as I float on my back, naked and happy. He's my anchor. My everything.

He always has been.

My father's best friend. My husband. My life.

Everything I need.

And more.

The End

DON'T BE SHY. COME FOLLOW ME...

I WON'T BITE UNLESS YOU ASK ME TO

www.OliviaTTurner.com

facebook.com/OliviaTTurnerAuthor

instagram.com/authoroliviatturner

goodreads.com/OliviaTTurner

amazon.com/author/oliviatturner

bookbub.com/authors/olivia-t-turner

SUN, SAND, AND SEDUCTION

BY OLIVIA T. TURNER

I watch him from the beach everyday.
Bodhi Slater cuts through the giant Hawaiian waves like he
was born to surf.
He's gorgeous.
That shaggy hair. Those dark eyes. *Mmmmmm….*

And his shredded tattooed body is pure perfection.

Every twist on his surfboard shows off a new ab muscle that I didn't even know existed.

I thought I was too large for him, but one look at me and this rich billionaire surfer becomes *obsessed*.

Who knew that Bodhi Slater likes his girls with curves?

He's a *possessive* alpha who owns the island and gets whatever he wants.

But what happens when all he wants is me?

Who's ready for the beach? Grab your bathing suit and a cold drink because you're about to spend some time in the sand with a hot Over The Top surfer with a possessive attitude and a big board!

Get it on Amazon

CHAPTER ONE OF SUN, SAND, AND SEDUCTION

Ruby

I SMILE WHEN I SPOT HIM.

He's lying on his board in the ocean next to his friend as the huge blue waves crash down in front of them. I can't see his face too well from the beach, but I'd recognize that bright pink surfboard anywhere. Only Bodhi Slater can rock a bright pink like that.

I sit down on the warm sand and dig my toes in deeper where it's cooler. The waves are big today, not the giants like last week, but big enough that the local surfers like Bodhi are having fun.

My breath catches as I watch him paddle forward as a wave begins to rise out of the ocean. He leaps up on his board and my body starts to tingle when I see him begin to surf the crest.

He crunches down low and I get treated to the gorgeous view of his shredded body. He doesn't have an ounce of fat on him and his arms are pure perfection under a layer of sexy tattoos. Every twist of his body shows off a new ab muscle that I didn't even know existed.

"He's wearing his light grey boardshorts today, Gamma," I whisper even though there's no one around me. I know it's crazy, but I still think she can hear me. If her soul is anywhere in this universe, it's beside me watching Bodhi surfing. That was our favorite thing to do, and Bodhi's grey boardshorts were always her favorite. She loved how his butt looked in them.

"Look at that ass," she would say as she slapped the armrest of her wheelchair. "If I was seventy years younger…"

I would always laugh until she cut her horny gaze and turned to me. "You're seventy years younger. What's your excuse?"

My excuse? A guy like Bodhi Slater would never talk to me. That's my excuse and it's always been a good one.

He owns Slater Surfboards. Not only do they make the best surfboards on planet earth, but they have the biggest clothing line in Maui. You can pick any hot girl with long tanned legs on any beach in Hawaii and there's a ninety-five percent chance that they're hiding their perfect tits in a Slater brand Sun, Sand, and Seduction bikini.

Gamma would always shake her head whenever I told her that going after the island's coolest and sexiest CEO would lead to nothing but embarrassment.

That woman did not believe in excuses. She came from a tough generation that took what they wanted. They made the United States into the powerhouse that it is today through sheer will and badassery. Nazis causing shit? All right, let's go kick their asses. Economy in the shitter? All right, let's roll up our sleeves and turn this ship around.

She was from the generation that went to the moon just because why the hell not? They laid down the railroad tracks and built the freeways that connected the country.

All we do is divide it by typing garbage into our phones

while driving over the broken roads that they built for us. Not even bothering to fix any of it.

Maybe I should be more like her… Gamma always was my favorite person.

Tears start to prickle my eyes as I grab a handful of sand and let it leak through my fingers. It's only been three weeks. It still hurts.

I still miss her so much.

Bodhi drops into the wave and my heart starts pounding when I see him start to ride it. He's so good. He's so fucking hot.

His light brown hair is just the right length of long and it blows in the wind as he goes. He hasn't shaved yet and his jaw is all scruffy—just the way I like it.

How many times have I fantasized about sliding my hands over those scruffy cheeks as he leaned down to kiss me?

Too many to count.

Bodhi puts his hand in the water and does a cutback, turning back into the power of the wave. I never take my eyes off him as he keeps riding it.

Every morning before work he's here, and every morning I'm here to watch him.

I've been in Maui for a year, but I've only missed the days that Gamma was really sick.

Just over a year ago, I was living in Pittsburgh. It was cold and snowy and gross and I had no job or boyfriend or life really. Gamma got sick. I was a wreck.

It was her idea to move down to Hawaii to spend the last days of her life in the sun and sand where she belonged and she asked me to come with her.

I didn't even have to think about it. My parents have always been no good and Gamma was always the one who looked out for me. She made sure I had shoes that fit and that my homework was always done. She lived in the unit above ours in the duplex that her and my grandfather bought and I spent every moment I could up there.

It was my sanctuary. It was my true home. And Gamma was my only real parent.

So when she asked me to come and live with her in Hawaii, I said yes immediately. It killed me that I might be living in a world without her and I wanted to spend as much time with her as I could, so I dropped what little I had and came down.

A part of me thinks that she did it for me. To get me out of my funk. To get me in the sun and sand and maybe even get me laid. Well, I've been in the sun and the sand, but that's about it. I'm a still a nineteen-year-old virgin living in paradise, but sad as fuck.

Watching Bodhi surf is the only thing that brings a smile to my face these days.

The wave runs out and he drops to his pink board and begins paddling back out when my phone rings.

Shit. My dad.

"Hello?"

"I got a buyer. I need you out of the house in three days."

My stomach drops and I'm struggling to breathe. Three days?

"But…"

"I need you to get all of Gamma's shit out of there. Today!"

I can feel my blood pressure starting to rise as my chest tightens. He knows it's supposed to be mine.

"Gamma was supposed to leave it for me, Dad. She told me."

Our little place that has the best views of the sunset in the world. A ten-minute walk to this spot. Gamma told me that she was going to arrange the will so I could have it when she was gone. She didn't want me to return to Pittsburgh any more than I wanted to go back.

"She was my mother, Ruby. All of her belongings go to me."

Not all of them. Only the ones he could trade for money.

"But I have nowhere else to stay. I have no job or money to rent an apartment."

I can hear the impatience and lack of shit giving in his annoyed breathing. *"Then come back to Pittsburgh. You can stay in your old room until you find a job."*

The thought makes me nauseous. I'd rather walk into the ocean and let those huge waves swallow me whole.

"But, Gamma told me—"

"I'm not going to argue about this with you!" my dad snaps. *"It's sold. I'm keeping the money. Either come back or don't. Just be out in three days."*

The line goes dead and all I can hear is the seagulls, the crashing of the waves, and the whistling of the wind as it blows into my hair.

I drop my phone back into my bag and look up at the blue sky.

"I wish you were still here."

There's no answer. There never is.

I'm starting to think that I'm completely on my own now.

It's a lonely feeling.

I turn back to Bodhi as he hops onto his pink board and catches another huge wave.

"At least I have you, Bodhi," I whisper to him even though he can't hear me. "I just wish you had me back."

CHAPTER TWO OF SUN, SAND, AND SEDUCTION

Bodhi

THE STRESS JUST MELTS OFF ME AS I RIDE THE CREST OF THE WAVE. The hot Hawaiian sun is on my face, the ocean is spraying me with a fine mist, and I'm feeling like a king as I stand on top of the best waves in the world.

I grin as I crouch down low, tilt my board into the wave, and fall into it. The wind whips through my hair and waters my eyes as I twist my hips to bring my board back up.

I come here every morning before work.

Surfing is my yoga, my meditation, my escape. I don't know where I'd be without it. Probably a wreck of tension and energy. Definitely not the founder and CEO of one of the island's biggest companies. I've always been wound really tight with an intense personality and surfing is the only thing that keeps me level and keeps me from snapping someone's neck.

Dylan says I need to get laid, but I've never had much of a need for that. I'm surrounded by beautiful women all day and they all want a piece of my rich ass, but I'm not interested in any of them. At the headquarters of my clothing brand—Sun, Surf, and Seduction—there are always gorgeous models walking the halls as well as professional female surfers who have the best bodies around. Best bodies for the ad campaigns—not for me. I like someone with a *real* body. Curves, beautiful flaws, sweet imperfections—those are the good stuff.

Nothing is more boring than perfect.

"There's a big one," Dylan shouts out once the wave has disappeared and I'm paddling back. "I'm taking it."

I shake my head when I see the size of it. He's not much of a surfer, but I like hanging around the guy. He's my CFO and best friend since childhood. He's lucky he helped me fight off Charlie Parker in the third grade when he was bullying me over a girl, otherwise, I would never keep him around the office. He's absolute shit at his job.

Good at banging the models though, but shit at handling the company's finances.

Dylan paddles out to the crest and hops up on his board. He doesn't even last five seconds before he falls off and tumbles down the edge.

I laugh as the wave comes crashing down on his head. The only surfing skill he has is that he can hold his breath for over four minutes. If not for that, he would have been dead a long time ago.

He pops up a few minutes later near the shore and I paddle out to catch one last wave before we have to get to work. We're about to launch a national marketing campaign for a new line of bikinis and we have the first photoshoot today. There are going to be models everywhere. Dylan is very excited. I'm dreading it.

The ocean starts to rise and I do my thing, paddling to the crest before jumping on my bright pink board and melting my stress away.

I'm riding it hard when I spot someone on the beach that yanks my attention away like a ripcord.

My chest tightens and I can't breathe as I stare at her. She's sitting crosslegged in the sand, watching me.

The warm breeze is dragging her wavy hair in front of her face as she grabs handfuls of sand in her tiny hands and lets it drain through her fingers.

She's fucking perfect.

Perfect.

Her gorgeous eyes look red and sad like she's trying not to cry and a surge of emotion swells inside of me. I want to know who made those sweet eyes tear up so I can find them and take their worthless lives for making my girl upset.

Listen to me… I'm already calling her *my* girl.

I'm an animal at heart and she's bringing the untamed side out of me. I want to rush over there and be by her side. Protect her. Comfort her. Breed her. I want it all.

She steals my attention and I'm so captivated by her that I can't pull my eyes away. Which is a bad thing when you're riding a ten-foot wave. My board catches the water and it sends me flying like a piece of seaweed. I hit the water hard and it knocks the breath out of my lungs right as the wave crashes down on my head.

It plunges me down deep into the ocean and viciously throws me around like a bug getting flushed down the toilet. I get thrown around every which way, but the turmoil of the crashing wave is nothing compared to what I'm feeling inside.

I swim hard to the surface for a breath. Not of air, but of her. She's the new air that I breathe. I *have* to see her again.

My head finally pops out of the water and I look around the beach with frantic eyes. I spot her, but she's standing up and picking up her bag. She wipes the sand off of her beautiful curvy ass as she takes one last look up and down the beach before heading toward the path out.

"No!" I shout. "Wait! Com—"

Another wave crashes on my head and I get a gallon of salty water shoved down my throat. *Fuck!*

I come up coughing and hacking up ocean water. I can barely breathe let alone call to her, so I just watch through my watery eyes. She's incredible.

I'm in a daze as I watch her walk along the beautiful Hawaiian beach like she's a goddess of sand and sun. She's in a bikini with a sarong wrapped around her waist, but she's not like all of the other perfect Barbie girls that are constantly buzzing around me like flies. She's thicker with a real woman's body. She's the girl I want for my ad campaign.

She's also the girl who I want to carry my child.

So many conflicting emotions are battling within me and I don't know how to handle any of it. It feels like I'm being torn apart from two directions.

I want to see her face on billboards, but at the same time, I want to keep her all to myself. I want everyone to see her beauty, but at the same time, I want to take the eyes of anyone who dares to look at her body.

I told you I was a little intense.

I'm a powerful man who gets what he wants and I just found the ultimate prize. The girl who I want to *own*.

And *nothing* is going to stop me from getting her. Except maybe for these relentless fucking waves.

Another one crashes down on my head while I'm distracted and Dylan is laughing his ass off when I finally come back up.

"You got wrecked, dude!"

He's paddling over on his board and dragging mine behind him. I grab onto it and float as I search the beach for her.

She's gone.

"Aren't you going to get on?" he asks with a chuckle.

I can't. My cock is rock hard and I don't know how to surf with a hard-on.

"You go ahead," I say as the world spins around me. "I need a second."

He shrugs and paddles off, leaving me as I try to compose myself. I've never had a reaction to a girl like that. Ever. And I've seen them all.

My dick isn't going down anytime soon, so I just hop on my board and get a tiny bit of relief by pressing my hard shaft against the board while I paddle back to shore.

I toss my board into the sand when I arrive and head straight to the spot where I saw her sitting. Her perfect ass is imprinted in the sand behind her cute little footprints.

I can feel drops of warm cum oozing out of my hard cock as I trace my fingertip around the footprint that's so small it could easily be a child's.

"Fuck."

I have to find her.

But how?

Go to www.OliviaTTurner.com to keep reading
Sun, Sand, and Seduction